Auguste Groner

The Case of the Lamp that Went out

Auguste Groner

The Case of the Lamp that Went out

ISBN/EAN: 9783955630287

Auflage: 1

Erscheinungsjahr: 2013

Erscheinungsort: Bremen, Deutschland

Leseklassiker

Contents

INTRODUCTION TO JOE MULLER

Joseph Muller, Secret Service detective of the Imperial Austrian police, is one of the great experts in his profession. In personality he differs greatly from other famous detectives. He has neither the impressive authority of Sherlock Holmes, nor the keen brilliancy of Monsieur Lecoq. Muller is a small, slight, plain-looking man, of indefinite age, and of much humbleness of mien. A naturally retiring, modest disposition, and two external causes are the reasons for Muller's humbleness of manner, which is his chief characteristic. One cause is the fact that in early youth a miscarriage of justice gave him several years in prison, an experience which cast a stigma on his name and which made it impossible for him, for many years after, to obtain honest employment. But the world is richer, and safer, by Muller's early misfortune. For it was this experience which threw him back on his own peculiar talents for a livelihood, and drove him into the police force. Had he been able to enter any other profession, his genius might have been stunted to a mere pastime, instead of being, as now, utilised for the public good.

Then, the red tape and bureaucratic etiquette which attaches to every governmental department, puts the secret service men of the Imperial police on a par with the lower ranks of the subordinates. Muller's official rank is scarcely much higher than that of a policeman, although kings and councillors consult him and the Police Department realises to the full what a treasure it has in him. But official red tape, and his early misfortune... prevent the giving of any higher official standing to even such a genius. Born and bred to such conditions, Muller understands them, and his natural modesty of disposition asks for no outward honours, asks for nothing but an income sufficient for his simple needs, and for aid and opportunity to occupy himself in the way he most enjoys.

Joseph Muller's character is a strange mixture. The kindest-hearted man in the world, he is a human bloodhound when once the lure of the trail has caught him. He scarcely eats or sleeps when the chase is on, he does not seem to know human weakness nor fatigue, in spite of his frail body. Once put on a case his mind delves and delves until it finds a clue, then something awakes within him, a spirit akin to that which holds the bloodhound nose to trail, and he will accomplish the apparently impossible, he will track down his victim when the entire machinery of a great police department seems helpless to discover anything. The high chiefs and commissioners grant a condescending permission when Muller asks, "May I do this? ... or may I handle this case this way?" both parties knowing all the while that it is a farce, and that the department waits helpless until this humble little man saves its honour by solving some problem before which its intricate machinery has stood dazed and puzzled.

This call of the trail is something that is stronger than anything else in Muller's mentality, and now and then it brings him into conflict with the department,... or with his own better nature. Sometimes his unerring instinct discovers secrets in high places, secrets which the Police Department is bidden to hush up and leave untouched. Muller is then taken off the case, and left idle for a while if he persists in his opinion as to the true facts. And at other times, Muller's own warm heart gets him into trouble. He will track down his victim, driven by the power in his soul which is stronger than all volition; but when he has this victim in the net, he will sometimes discover him to be a much finer, better man than the other individual, whose wrong at this particular criminal's hand set in motion the machinery of justice. Several times that has happened to Muller, and each time his heart got the better of his professional instincts, of his practical common-sense, too, perhaps,... at least as far as his own advancement was concerned, and he warned the victim, defeating his own work. This peculiarity of Muller's character caused his undoing at last, his official undoing that is, and compelled his retirement from the force. But his advice is often sought unofficially by the Department, and to those who know, Muller's hand can be seen in the unravelling of many a famous case.

The following stories are but a few of the

many interesting cases that have come within the experience of this great detective. But they give a fair portrayal of Muller's peculiar method of working, his looking on himself as merely an humble member of the Department, and the comedy of his acting under "official orders" when the Department is in reality following out his directions.

THE CASE OF THE LAMP THAT WENT OUT

CHAPTER I. THE DISCOVERY

The radiance of a clear September morning lay over Vienna. The air was so pure that the sky shone in brightest azure even where the city's buildings clustered thickest. On the outskirts of the town the rays of the awakening sun danced in crystalline ether and struck answering gleams from the dew on grass and shrub in the myriad gardens of the suburban streets.

It was still very early. The old-fashioned steeple clock on the church of the Holy Virgin in Hietzing had boomed out six slow strokes but a short time back. Anna, the pretty blonde girl who carried out the milk for the dwellers in several streets of this aristocratic residential suburb, was just coming around the corner of the main street into a quiet lane. This lane could hardly be dignified by the name of street as yet, it was so very quiet. It had been opened and named scarcely a year back and it was bordered mostly by open gardens or fenced-in building lots. There were four houses in this street, two by two opposite each other, and another, an old-fashioned manor house, lying almost hidden in its great garden. But the quiet street could not presume to ownership of this last house, for the front of it opened on a parallel street, which gave it its number. Only the garden had a gate as outlet onto our quiet lane.

Anna stopped in front of this gate and pulled the bell. She had to wait for some little time until the gardener's wife, who acted as janitress, could open the door. But Anna was not impatient, for she knew that it was quite a distance from the gardener's house in the centre of the great stretch of park to the little gate where she waited. In a few moments, however, the door was opened and a pleasant-faced woman exchanged a friendly greeting with the girl and took the cans from her.

Anna hastened onward with her usual energetic step. The four houses in that street were already served and she was now bound for the homes of customers several squares away. Then her step slowed just a bit. She was a quiet, thoughtful girl and the lovely peace of this bright morning sank into her heart and made her rejoice in its beauty. All around her the foliage was turning gently to its autumn glory of colouring and the dewdrops on the rich-hued leaves sparkled with an unusual radiance. A thrush looked down at her from a bough and began its morning song. Anna smiled up at the little bird and began herself to sing a merry tune.

But suddenly her voice died away, the colour faded from her flushed cheeks, her eyes opened wide and she stood as if riveted to the ground. With a deep breath as of unconscious terror she let the burden of the milk cans drop gently from her shoulder to the ground. In following the bird's flight her eyes had wandered to the side of the street, to the edge of one of the vacant lots, there where a shallow ditch separated it from the roadway. An elder-tree, the great size of which attested its age, hung its berry-laden branches over the ditch. And in front of this tree the bird had stopped suddenly, then fluttered off with the quick movement of the wild creature surprised by fright. What the bird had seen was the same vision that halted the song on Anna's lips and arrested her foot. It was the body of a man — a young and well-dressed man, who lay there with his face turned toward the street. And his face was the white frozen face of a corpse.

Anna stood still, looking down at him for a few moments, in wide-eyed terror: then she walked on slowly as if trying to pull herself together again. A few steps and then she turned and broke into a run. When she reached the end of the street, breathless from haste and excitement, she found herself in one of the main arteries of traffic of the suburb, but owing to the early hour this street was almost as quiet as the lane she had just left. Finally the frightened girl's eyes caught sight of the figure of a policeman coming around the next corner. She flew to meet him and recognised him as the officer of that beat.

"Why, what is the matter?" he asked. "Why are you so excited?"

"Down there-in the lane, there's a dead man," answered the girl, gasping for breath.

"A dead man?" repeated the policeman gravely, looking at the girl. "Are you sure he's dead?"

Anna nodded. "His eyes are all glassy and I saw blood on his back."

"Well, you're evidently very much frightened, and I suppose you don't want to go down there again. I'll look into the matter, if you will go to the police station and make the announcement. Will you do it?"

"Yes, sir."

"All right, then, that will gain time for us. Good-bye, Miss Anna."

The man walked quickly down the street, while the girl hurried off in the opposite direction, to the nearest police station, where she told what she had seen.

The policeman reached his goal even earlier. The first glance told him that the man lying there by the wayside was indeed lifeless. And the icy stiffness of the hand which he touched showed him that life must have fled many hours back. Anna had been right about the blood also. The dead man lay on the farther side of the ditch, half down into it. His right arm was bent under his body, his left arm was stretched out, and the stiffened fingers... they were slender white fingers... had sought for something to break his fall. All they had found was a tall stem of wild aster with its purple blossoms, which they were holding fast in the death grip. On the dead man's back was a small bullet-wound and around the edges of it his light grey coat was stained with blood. His face was distorted in pain and terror. It was a nice face, or would have been, did it not show all too plainly the marks of dissipation in spite of the fact that the man could not have been much past thirty years old. He was a stranger to the policeman, although the latter had been on this beat for over three years.

When the guardian of the law had convinced himself that there was nothing more to do for the man who lay there, he rose from his stooping position and stepped back. His gaze wandered up and down the quiet lane, which was still absolutely empty of human life. He stood there quietly waiting, watching over the ghastly discovery. In about ten minutes the police commissioner and the coroner, followed by two roundsmen with a litter, joined the solitary watcher, and the latter could return to his post.

The policemen set down their litter and waited for orders, while the coroner and the commissioner bent over the corpse. There was nothing for the physician to do but to declare that the unfortunate man had been dead for many hours. The bullet which struck him in the back had killed him at once. The commissioner examined the ground immediately around the corpse, but could find nothing that pointed to a struggle.

There remained only to prove whether there had been a robbery as well as a murder.

"Judging from the man's position the bullet must have come from that direction," said the commissioner, pointing towards the cottages down the lane.

"People who are killed by bullets may turn several times before they fall," said a gentle voice behind the police officer. The voice seemed to suit the thin little man who stood there meekly, his hat in his hand.

The commissioner turned quickly. "Ah, are you there already, Muller?" he said, as if greatly pleased, while the physician broke in with the remark:

"That's just what I was about to observe. This man did not die so quickly that he could not have made a voluntary or involuntary movement before life fled. The shot that killed him might have come from any direction."

The commissioner nodded thoughtfully and there was silence for a few moments. Muller — for the little thin man was none other than the celebrated Joseph Muller, one of the most brilliant detectives in the service of the Austrian police — looked down at the corpse carefully.. He took plenty of time to do it and nobody hurried him. For nobody ever hurried Muller; his well-known and almost laughable thoroughness and pedantry were too valuable in their results. It was a tradition in the police that Muller was to have all the time he wanted for everything. It paid in the end, for Muller made few mistakes. Therefore, his superior the police commissioner, and the coroner waited quietly while the little man made his inspection of the corpse.

"Thank you," said Muller finally, with a polite bow to the commissioner, before he bent to brush away the dust on his knees.

"Well?" asked Commissioner Holzer.

Muller smiled an embarrassed smile as he replied:

"Well... I haven't found out anything yet except that he is dead, and that he has been shot in the back. His pockets may tell us something more."

"Yes, we can examine them at once," said the commissioner. "I have been delaying that for I wanted you here; but I had no idea that you would come so soon. I told them to fetch you if you were awake, but doubted you would be, for I know you have had no sleep for forty-eight hours."

"Oh, I can sleep, at least with one eye, when I'm on the chase," answered the detective. "So it's really only twenty-four hours, you see." Muller had just returned from tracking down an aristocratic swindler whom he had found finally in a little French city and had brought back to a Viennese prison. He had returned well along in the past night and Holzer knew that the tired man would need his rest. Still he had sent for Muller, who lived near the police station, for the girl's report had warned him that this was a serious case. And in serious cases the police did not like to do without Muller's help.

And as usual when his work called him, Muller was as wide awake as if he had had a good night's sleep behind him. The interest of a new case robbed him of every trace of fatigue. It was he alone — at his own request — who raised the body and laid it on its back before he stepped aside to make way for the doctor.

The physician opened the dead man's vest to see whether the bullet had passed completely through the body. But it had not; there was not the slightest trace of blood upon the shirt.

"There's nothing more for me to do here, Muller," said the physician, as he bowed to the commissioner and left the place.

Muller examined the pockets of the dead man.

"It's probably a case of robbery, too," re- marked the commissioner. "A man as well- dressed as this one is would be likely to have a watch."

"And a purse," added the detective. "But this man has neither — or at least he has them no longer."

In the various pockets of the dead man's clothes Muller found the following articles: a handkerchief, several tramway tickets, a penknife, a tiny mirror, and comb, and a little book, a cheap novel. He wrapped them all in the handkerchief and put them in his own pocket. The dead man's coat had fallen back from his body during the examination, and as Muller turned the stiffened limbs a little he saw the opening of another pocket high up over the right hip of the trousers. The detective passed his hand over the pocket and heard something rattle. Then he put his hand in the pocket and drew out a thin narrow envelope which he handed to the commissioner. Holzer looked at it carefully. It was made of very thin expensive paper and bore no address. But it was sealed, although not very carefully, for the gummed edges were open in spots. It must have been hastily closed and was slightly crushed as if it had been carried in a clenched hand. The commissioner cut open the envelope with his penknife. He gave an exclamation of surprise as he showed Muller the contents. In the envelope there were three hundred-gulden notes.

The commissioner looked at Muller without a word, but the detective understood and shook his head. "No," he said calmly, "it may be a case of robbery just the same. This pocket was not very easy to find, and the money in it was safer than the dead man's watch and purse would be. That is, if he had a watch and purse — and he very probably had a watch," he added more quickly.

For Muller had made a little discovery. On the lower hem of the left side of the dead man's waistcoat he saw a little lump, and feeling of it he discovered that it was a watch key which had slipped down out of the torn pocket between the lining and the material of the vest. A sure proof that the dead man had had a watch, which in all probability had been taken from him by his murderer. There was no loose change or small bills to be found in any of the pockets, so that it was more than likely that the dead man had had his money in a purse. It seemed to be a case of murder for the sake of robbery. At least Muller and the commissioner believed it to be one, from what they had discovered thus far.

The police officer gave his men orders to raise the body and to take it to the morgue. An hour later the unknown man lay in the bare room in which the only spot of brightness were the rays of the sun that crept through the high barred windows and touched his cold face and stiffened form as with a pitying caress. But no, there was one other little spot of brightness in the silent place. It was the wild aster which the dead man's hand still held tightly clasped. The little purple flowers were quite fresh yet, and the dewdrops clinging to them greeted the kiss of the sun's rays with an answering smile.

CHAPTER II. THE BROKEN WILLOW TWIG

As soon as the corpse had been taken away, the police commissioner returned to the station. But Muller remained there all alone to make a thorough examination of the entire vicinity.

It was not a very attractive spot, this particular part of the street. There must have been a nursery there at one time, for there were still several ordered rows of small trees to be seen. There were traces of flower cultivation as well, for several trailing vines and overgrown bushes showed where shrubs had been grown which do not usually grow without man's assistance. Immediately back of the old elder tree Muller found several fine examples of rare flowers, or rather he found the shrubs which his experienced eye recognised as having once borne these unusual blossoms. One or two blooms still hung to the bushes and the detective, who was a great lover of flowers, picked them and put them in his buttonhole. While he did this, his keen eyes were darting about the place taking in all the details. This vacant lot had evidently been used as an unlicensed dumping ground for some time, for all sorts of odds and ends, old boots, bits of stuff, silk and rags, broken bottles and empty tin cans, lay about between the bushes or half buried in the earth. What had once been an orderly garden was now an untidy receptacle for waste. The pedantically neat detective looked about him in disgust, then suddenly he forgot his displeasure and a gleam shot up in his eye. It was very little, the thing this man had seen, this man who saw so much more than others.

About ten paces from where he stood a high wooden fence hemmed in the lot. The fence belonged to the neighbouring property, as the lot in which he stood was not protected in any way. To the back it was closed off by a corn field where the tall stalks rustled gently in the faint morning breeze. All this could be seen by anybody and Muller had seen it all at his first glance. But now he had seen something else. Something that excited him because it might possibly have some connection with the newly discovered crime. His keen eyes, in glancing along the wooden fence at his right hand, had caught sight of a little twig which had worked its way through the fence. This twig belonged to a willow tree which grew on the other side, and which spread its grey-green foliage over the fence or through its wide openings. One of the little twigs which had crept in between the planks was broken, and it had been broken very recently, for the leaves were still fresh and the sap was oozing from the crushed stem. Muller walked over to the fence and examined the twig carefully. He soon saw how it came to be broken. The broken part was about the height of a man's knee from the ground. And just at this height there was quite a space between two of the planks of the fence, heavy planks which were laid cross-ways and nailed to thick posts. It would have been very easy for anybody to get a foothold in this open space between the planks.

It was very evidently some foot thrust in between the planks which had broken the little willow twig, and its soft rind had left a green mark on the lower plank. "I wonder if that has anything to do with the murder," thought Muller, looking over the fence into the lot on the other side.

This neighbouring plot was evidently a neglected garden. It had once worn an aristocratic air, with stone statues and artistic arrangement of flower beds and shrubs. It was still attractive even in its neglected condition. Beyond it, through the foliage of its heavy trees, glass windows caught the sunlight. Muller remembered that there was a handsome old house in this direction, a house with a mansard roof and wide-reaching wings. He did not now know to whom this handsome old house belonged, a house that must have been built in the time of Maria Theresa,... but he was sure of one thing, and that was that he would soon find out to whom it belonged. At present it was the garden which interested him, and he was anxious to see where it ended. A few moments' further inspection showed him what he wanted to know. The garden extended to the beginning of the park-like grounds which surrounded the old house with the mansard roof. A tall iron railing separated the garden from the park, but this railing did not extend down as far as the quiet lane. Where it ended there was a light, well-built wooden fence. Along the street side of the fence there was a high thick hedge. Muller walked along this hedge until he came to a little gate. Then crossing the street, he saw that the house whose windows glistened in the sunlight was a house which he knew well from its other side, its front facade.

Now he went back to the elder tree and then walked slowly away from this to the spot where he found the broken willow twig. He examined every foot of the ground, but there was nothing to be seen that was of any interest to him-not a foot-print, or anything to prove that some one else had passed that way a short time before. And yet it would have been impossible to pass that way without leaving some trace, for the ground was cut up in all directions by mole hills.

Next the detective scrutinised as much of the surroundings as would come into immediate con-nection with the spot where the corpse had been found. There was nothing to be seen there either, and Muller was obliged to acknowledge that he had discovered nothing that would lead to an understanding of the crime, unless, indeed, the broken willow twig should prove to be a clue. He sprang back across the ditch, turned up the edges of his trousers where they had been moistened by the dew and walked slowly along the dusty street. He was no longer alone in the lane. An old man, accompanied by a large dog, came out from one of the new houses and walked towards the detective, he was very evidently going in the direction of the elder-tree, which had already been such a centre of interest that morning. When he met Muller, the old man halted, touched his cap and asked in a confidential tone: "I suppose you've been to see the place already?"

"Which place?" was Muller's reserved answer.

"Why, I mean the place where they found the man who was murdered. They found him under that elder-tree. My wife just heard of it and told me. I suppose everybody round here will know it soon."

"Was there a man murdered here?" asked Muller, as if surprised by the news.

"Yes, he was shot last night. Only I don't understand why I didn't hear the shot. I couldn't sleep a wink all night for the pain in my bones."

"You live near here, then?"

"Yes, I live in No.1. Didn't you see me coming out?"

"I didn't notice it. I came across the wet meadows and I stooped to turn up my trousers so that they wouldn't get dusty — it must have been then you came out."

"Why, then you must have been right near the place I was talking about. Do you see that elder tree there? It's the only one in the street, and the girl who brings the milk found the man under it. The police have been here already and have taken him away. They discovered him about six o'clock and now it's just seven."

"And you hadn't any suspicion that this dreadful thing was happening so near you?" asked the detective casually.

"I didn't know a thing, sir, not a thing. There couldn't have been a fight or I would have heard it. But I don't know why I didn't hear the shot."

"Why, then you must have been asleep after all, in spite of your pain," said Muller with a smile, as he walked along beside the man back to the place from which he had just come.

The old man shook his head. "No, I tell you I didn't close an eye all night. I went to bed at half-past nine and I smoked two pipes before I put out the light, and then I heard every hour strike all night long and it wasn't until nearly five o'clock, when it was almost dawn, that I dozed off a bit."

"Then it is astonishing that you didn't hear anything!"

"Sure it's astonishing! But it's still more as-tonishing that my dog Sultan didn't hear any-thing. Sultan is a famous watchdog, I'd have you know. He'll growl if anybody passes through the street after dark, and I don't see why he didn't notice what was going on over there last night. If a man's attacked, he generally calls for help; it's a queer business all right."

"Well, Sultan, why didn't you make a noise?" asked Muller, patting the dog's broad head. Sultan growled and walked on indifferently, after he had shaken off the strange hand.

"He must have slept more soundly than usual. He went off into the country with me yesterday. We had an errand to do there and on the way back we stopped in for a drink. Sultan takes a drop or two himself occasionally, and that usually makes him sleep. I had hard work to bring him home. We got here just a few minutes before half-past nine and I tell you we were both good and tired."

By this time they had come to the elder-tree and the old man's stream of talk ceased as he stood before the spot where the mysterious crime had occurred. He looked down thoughtfully at the grass, now trampled by many feet. "Who could have done it?" he murmured finally, with a sigh that expressed his pity for the victim.

"Hietzing is known to be one of the safest spots in Vienna," remarked Muller.

"Indeed it is, sir; indeed it is. As it would well have to be with the royal castles right here in the neighbourhood! Indeed it would have to be safe with the Court coming here all the time."

"Why, yes, you see more police here than anywhere else in the city."

"Yes, they're always sticking their nose in where they're not necessary," remarked the old man, not realising to whom he was speaking. "They fuss about everything you do or don't do, and yet a man can be shot down right under our very noses here and the police can't help it."

"But, my dear sir, it isn't always possible for the police to prevent a criminal carrying out his evil intention," said Muller good-naturedly.

"Well, why not? if they watch out sharp enough?"

"The police watch out sharper than most people think. But they can't catch a man until he has committed his crime, can they?"

"No, I suppose not," said the old man, with another glance at the elder-tree. He bowed to Muller and turned and walked away.

Muller followed him slowly, very much pleased with this meeting, for it had given him a new clue. There was no reason to doubt the old man's story. And if this story was true, then the crime had been committed before half-past nine of the evening previous. For the old man — he was evidently the janitor in No.1 — had not heard the shot.

Muller left the scene of the crime and walked towards the four houses. Before he reached them he had to pass the garden which belonged to the house with the mansard roof. Right and left of this garden were vacant lots, as well as on the opposite side of the street. Then came to the right and left the four new houses which stood at the beginning of the quiet lane. Muller passed them, turned up a cross street and then down again, into the street running parallel, to the lane, a quiet aristocratic street on which fronted the house with the mansard roof.

A carriage stood in front of this house, two great trunks piled up on the box beside the driver. A young girl and an old man in livery were placing bags and bundles of rugs inside the carriage. Muller walked slowly toward the carriage. Just as he reached the open gate of the garden he was obliged to halt, to his own great satisfaction. For at this moment a group of people came out from the house, the owners of it evidently, prepared for a journey and surrounded by their servants.

Beside the old man and the young girl, there were two other women, one evidently the housekeeper, the other possibly the cook. The latter was weeping openly and devoutly kissing the hand of her mistress. The housekeeper discovered that a rug was missing and sent the maid back for it, while the old servant helped the lady into the carriage. The door of the carriage was wide open and Muller had a good glimpse of the pale, sweet-faced and delicate-looking young women who leaned back in her corner, shivering and evidently ill. The servants bustled about, making her comfortable, while her husband superintended the work with anxious tenderness. He was a tall, fine-looking man with deep-set grey eyes and a rich, sympathetic voice. He gave his orders to his servants with calm authority, but he also was evidently suffering from the disease of our century – nervousness, for Muller saw that the man's hands clenched feverishly and that his lips were trembling under his drooping moustache.

The maid hastened down with the rug and spread it over her mistress's knees, as the gentleman exclaimed nervously: "Do hurry with that! Do you want us to miss the train?"

The butler closed the door of the carriage, the coachman gathered up the reins and raised his whip. The housekeeper bowed low and murmured a few words in farewell and the other servants followed her example with tears in their eyes. "You'll see us again in six weeks," the lady called out and her husband added: "If all goes well." Then he motioned to the waiting driver and the carriage moved off swiftly, turning the corner in a few moments.

The little group of servants returned to the courtyard behind the high gates. Muller, whom they had not noticed, was about to resume his walk, when he halted again. The courtyard of the house led back through a flagged walk to the park-like garden that surrounded it on the sides and rear. Down this walk came a young woman. She came so quickly that one might almost call it running. She was evidently excited about something. Muller imagined what this something might be, and he remained to hear what she had to say. He was not mistaken. The woman, it was Mrs. Schmiedler, the gardener's wife, began her story at once. "Haven't you heard yet?" she said breathlessly. "No, you can't have heard it yet or you wouldn't stand there so quietly, Mrs. Bernauer."

"What's the matter?" asked the woman whom Muller took to be the housekeeper.

"They killed a man last night out here! They found his body just now in the lane back of our garden. The janitor from No.1 told me as I was going to the store, so I went right back to look at the place, and I came to tell you, as I didn't think you'd heard it yet."

Mrs. Bernauer was evidently a woman of strong constitution and of an equable mind. The other three servants broke out into an excited hubbub of talk while she remained quite indifferent and calm. "One more poor fellow who had to leave the world before he was ready," she remarked calmly, with just the natural touch of pity in her voice that would come to any warmhearted human being upon hearing of such an occurrence. She did not seem at all excited or alarmed to think that the scene of the crime had been so near.

The other servants were very much more excited and had already rushed off, under the guidance of the gardener's wife, to look at the dreadful spot. Franz, the butler, had quite forgotten to close the front gate in his excitement, and the housekeeper turned to do it now.

"The fools, see them run," she exclaimed half aloud. "As if there was anything for them to do there."

The gate closed, Mrs. Bernauer turned and walked slowly to the house. Muller walked on also, going first to the police station to report what he had discovered. Then he went to his own rooms and slept until nearly noon. On his return to the police station he found that notices of the occurrence had already been sent out to the papers.

CHAPTER III. THE EVENING PAPER

The autopsy proved beyond a doubt that the murdered man had been dead for many hours before the discovery of his body. The bullet which had struck him in the back had pierced the trachea and death had occurred within a few minutes. The only marks for identification of the body were the initials L. W. on his underwear. The evening paper printed an exact description of the man's appearance and his clothing.

It was about ten o'clock next morning when Mrs. Klingmayer, a widow living in a quiet street at the opposite end of the city from Hietzing, returned from her morning marketing. It was only a few little bundles that she brought with her and she set about preparing her simple dinner. Her packages were wrapped in newspapers, which she carefully smoothed out and laid on the dresser.

Mrs. Klingmayer was the widow of a streetcar conductor and the little pension which she received from the company, as well as the money she could earn for herself, did not permit of the indulgence in a daily newspaper. And yet the reading of the papers was the one luxury for which the simple woman longed. Her grocer, who was a friend of years, knew this and would wrap up her purchases in papers of recent date, knowing that she could then enjoy them in her few moments of leisure. To-day this leisure came unexpectedly early, for Mrs. Klingmayer had less work than usual to attend to.

Her little flat consisted of two rooms and a kitchen with a large closet opening out from it. She lived in the kitchen and rented the front rooms. Her tenants were a middle-aged man, inspector in a factory, who had the larger room; and a younger man who was bookkeeper in an importing house in the city. But this young man had not been at home for forty-eight hours, a fact, however, which did not greatly worry his landlady. The gentleman in question lived a rather dissipated life and it was not the first time that he had remained away from home over night. It is true that it was the first time that he had not been home for two successive nights. But as Mrs. Klingmayer thought, everything has to happen the first time sometime. "It's not likely to be the last time," the worthy woman thought.

At all events she was rather glad of it to-day, for she suffered from rheumatism and it was difficult for her to get about. The young man's absence saved her the work of fixing up his room that morning and allowed her to get to her reading earlier than usual. When she had put the pot of soup on the fire, she sat down by the window, adjusted her big spectacles and began to read. To her great delight she discovered that the paper she held in her hand bore the date of the previous afternoon. In spite of the good intentions of her friend the grocer, it was not always that she could get a paper of so recent date, and she began to read with doubled anticipation of pleasure.

She did not waste time on the leading articles, for she understood little about politics. The serial stories were a great delight to her, or would have been, if she had ever been able to follow them consecutively. But her principal joy were the everyday happenings of varied interest which she found in the news columns. To-day she was so absorbed in the reading of them that the soup pot began to boil over and send out rivulets down onto the stove. Ordinarily this would have shocked Mrs. Klingmayer, for the neatness of her pots and pans was the one great care of her life. But now, strange to relate, she paid no attention to the soup, nor to the smell and the smoke that arose from the stove. She had just come upon a notice in the paper which took her entire attention. She read it through three times, and each time with growing excitement. This is what she read:

MURDER IN HIETZING

This morning at six o'clock the body of a man about 30 years old was discovered in a lane in Hietzing. The man must have been dead many hours. He had been shot from behind. The dead man was tall and thin, with brown eyes, brown hair and moustache. The letters L. W. were embroidered in his underwear. There was nothing else discovered on him that could reveal his identity. His watch and purse were not in his pockets: presumably they had been taken by the murderer. A strange fact is that in one of his pockets — a hidden pocket it is true — there was the sum of 300 guldens in bills.

This was the notice which made Mrs. Klingmayer neglect the soup pot.

Finally the old woman stood up very slowly, threw a glance at the stove and opened the window mechanically. Then she lifted the pots from the fire and set them on the outer edge of the range. And then she did something that ordinarily would have shocked her economical soul — she poured water on the fire to put it out.

When she saw that there was not a spark left in the stove, she went into her own little room and prepared to go out. Her excitement caused her to forget her rheumatism entirely. One more look around her little kitchen, then she locked it up and set out for the centre of the city.

She went to the office of the importing house where her tenant, Leopold Winkler, was employed as bookkeeper. The clerk at the door noticed the woman's excitement and asked her kindly what the trouble was.

"I'd like to speak to Mr. Winkler," she said eagerly.

"Mr. Winkler hasn't come in yet," answered the young man. "Is anything the matter? You look so white! Winkler will probably show up soon, he's never very punctual. But it's after eleven o'clock now and he's never been as late as this before."

"I 'don't believe he'll ever come again," said the old woman, sinking down on a bench beside the 'door.

"Why, what do you mean?" asked the clerk. "Why shouldn't he come again?"

"Is the head of the firm here?" asked Mrs. Klingmayer, wiping her forehead with her handkerchief. The clerk nodded and hurried away to tell his employer about the woman with the white face who came to ask for a man who, as she expressed it, "would never come there again."

"I don't think she's quite right in the head," he volunteered. The head of the firm told him to bring the woman into the inner office.

"Who are you, my good woman?" he asked kindly, softened by the evident agitation of this poorly though neatly dressed woman.

"I am Mr. Winkler's landlady," she answered.

"Ah! and he wants you to tell me that he's sick? I'm afraid I can't believe all that this gentleman says. I hope he's not asking your help to lie to me. Are you sure that his illness is anything else but a case of being up late?"

"I don't think that he'll ever be sick again — I didn't come with any message from him, sir; please read this, sir." And she handed him the newspaper, showing him the notice. While the gentleman was reading she added: "Mr. Winkler didn't come home last night either."

Winkler's employer read the few lines, then laid the paper aside with a very serious face. "When did you see him last?" he asked of the woman.

"Day before yesterday in the morning. He went away about half-past eight as he usually does," she replied. And then she added a question of her own: "Was he here day before yesterday?"

The merchant nodded and pressed an electric bell. Then he rose from his seat and pulled up a chair for his visitor. "Sit down here. This thing has frightened you and you are no longer young." When the servant entered, the merchant told him to ask the head bookkeeper to come to the inner office.

When this official appeared, his employer inquired: "When did Winkler leave here day before yesterday?"

"At six o'clock, sir, as usual."

"He was here all day without interruption?"

"Yes, sir, with the exception of the usual luncheon hour."

"Did he have the handling of any money Monday?"

"No, sir."

"Thank you, Mr. Pokorny," said the merchant, handing his employee the evening paper and pointing to the notice which had so interested him.

Pokorny read it, his face, like his employer's, growing more serious. "It looks almost as if it must be Winkler, sir," he said, in a few moments.

"We will soon find that out. I should like to go to the police station myself with this woman; she is Winkler's landlady — but I think it will be better for you to accompany her. They will ask questions about the man which you will be better able to answer than I."

Pokorny bowed and left the room. Mrs. Klingmayer rose and was about to follow, when the merchant asked her to wait a moment and inquired whether Winkler owed her anything. "I am sorry that you should have had this shock and the annoyances and trouble which will come of it, but I don't want you to be out of pocket by it."

"No, he doesn't owe me anything," replied the honest old woman, shaking her head. A few big tears rolled down over her withered cheeks, possibly the only tears that were shed for the dead man under the elder-tree. But even this sympathetic soul could find nothing to say in his praise. She could feel pity for his dreadful death, but she could not assert that the world had lost anything by his going out of it. As if saddened by the impossibility of finding a single good word to say about the dead man, she left the office with drooping head and lagging step.

Pokorny helped her into the cab that was already waiting before the door. The office force had got wind of the fact that something unusual had occurred and were all at the windows to see them drive off. The three clerks who worked in the department to which Winkler belonged gathered together to talk the matter over. They were none of them particularly hit by it, but naturally they were interested in the discovery in Hietzing, and equally naturally, they tried to find a few good words to say about the man whose life had ended so suddenly.

The youngest of them, Fritz Bormann, said some kind words and was about to wax more enthusiastic, when Degenhart, the eldest clerk, cut in with the words: "Oh, don't trouble yourself. Nobody ever liked Winkler here. 'He was not a good man — he was not even a good worker. This is the first time that he has a reasonable excuse for neglecting his duties."

"Oh, come, see here! how can you talk about the poor man that way when he's scarcely cold in death yet," said Fritz indignantly.

Degenhart laughed harshly.

"Did I ever say anything else about him while he was warm and alive? Death is no reason for changing one's opinion about a man who was good-for-nothing in life. And his death was a stroke of good luck that he scarcely deserved. He died without a moment's pain, with a merry thought in his head, perhaps, while many another better man has to linger in torture for weeks. No, Bormann, the best I can say about Winkler is that his death makes one nonentity the less on earth."

The older man turned to his desk again and the two younger clerks continued the conversation: "Degenhart appears to be a hard man," said Fritz, "but he's the best and kindest person I know, and he's dead right in what he says. It was simply a case of conventional superstition. I never did like that Winkler."

"No, you're right," said the other. "Neither did I and I don't know why, for the matter of that. He seemed just like a thousand others. I never heard of anything particularly wrong that he did."

"No, no more did I," continued Bormann, "but I never heard of anything good about him either. And don't you think that it's worse for a man to seem to repel people by his very personality, rather than by any particular bad thing that he does?"

"Yes. I don't know how to explain it, but that's just how I feel about it. I had an instinctive feeling that there was something wrong about Winkler, the sort of a creepy, crawly feeling that a snake gives you."

CHAPTER IV. SPEAK WELL OF THE DEAD

Meanwhile Pokomy and Mrs. Klingmayer had reached the police station and were going upstairs to the rooms of the commissioner on service for the day. Like all people of her class, Mrs. Klingmayer stood in great awe and terror of anything connected with the police or the law generally. She crept slowly and tremblingly up the stairs behind the head bookkeeper and was very glad when she was left alone for a few minutes while Pokorny went in to see the commissioner. But as soon as his errand was known, both the bookkeeper and his companion were led into the office of Head Commissioner Dr. von Riedau, who had charge of the Hietzing murder case.

When Dr. von Riedau heard the reason of their coming, his interest was immediately aroused, and he pulled a chair to his side for the little thin man with whom he had been talking when the two strangers were ushered in.

"Then you believe you could identify the murdered man?" asked the commissioner.

"From the general description and the initials on his linen, I believe it must be Leopold Winkler," answered Pokorny. "Mrs. Klingmayer has not seen him since Monday morning, nor has she had any message from him. He left the office Monday afternoon at 6 o'clock and that was the last time that we saw him. The only thing that makes me doubt his identity is that the paper reports that three hundred gulden were found in his pocket. Winkler never seemed to have money, and I do not understand how he should have been in possession of such a sum."

"The money was found in the dead man's pockets," said the commissioner. "And yet it may be Winkler, the man you know. Muller, will you order a cab, please?"

"I have a cab waiting for me. But it only holds two," volunteered Pokorny.

"That doesn't matter, I'll sit on the box," answered the man addressed as Muller.

"You are going with us?" asked Pokorny.

"Yes, he will accompany you," replied the commissioner. "This is detective Muller, sir. By a mere chance, he happened to be on hand to take charge of this case and he will remain in charge, although it may be wasting his talents which we need for more difficult problems. If you or any one else have anything to tell us, it must be told only to me or to Muller. And before you leave to look at the body, I would like to know whether the dead man owned a watch, or rather whether he had it with him on the day of the murder."

"Yes, sir; he did have a watch, a gold watch," answered Mrs. Klingmayer.

Riedau looked at the bookkeeper, who nodded and said: "Yes, sir; Winkler had a watch, a gold watch with a double case. It was a large watch, very thick. I happen to have noticed it by chance and also I happen to know that he had not had the watch for very long."

"Can you tell us anything more about the watch?" asked the commissioner of the landlady.

"Yes, sir; there was engraving on the outside cover, initials, and a crown on the other side."

"What were the initials?"

"I don't know that, sir; at least I'm not sure about it. There were so many twists and curves to them that I couldn't make them out. I think one of them was a W though, sir."

"The other was probably an L then."

"That might be, sir."

"The younger clerks in the office may be able to tell something more about the watch," said Pokorny, "for they were quite interested in it for a while. It was a handsome watch and they were envious of Winkler's possession of it. But he was so tactless in his boasting about it that they paid no further attention to him after the first excitement."

"You say he didn't have the watch long?"

"Since spring I think, sir."

"He brought it home on the 19th of March," interrupted Mrs. Klingmayer. "I remember the day because it was my birthday. I pretended that he had brought it home to me for a present."

"Was he in the habit of making you presents?"

"Oh, no, sir; he was very close with his money, sir.

"Well, perhaps he didn't have much money to be generous with. Now tell me about his watch chain. I suppose he had a watch chain?"

Both the bookkeeper and the landlady nodded and the latter exclaimed: "Oh, yes, sir; I could recognise it in a minute."

"How?"

"It was broken once and Mr. Winkler mended it himself. I lent him my pliers and he bent the two links together with them. It didn't look very nice after that, but it was strong again. You could see the mark of the pliers easily."

"Why didn't he take the chain to the jeweler's to be fixed?" asked the commissioner.

The woman smiled. "It wouldn't have been worth the money, sir; the chain wasn't real gold."

"But the watch was real, wasn't it?"

"Oh, yes, sir; that was real gold. I pawned it once for Mr. Winkler and they gave me 24 gulden for it."

"One question more, did he have a purse? And did he have it with him on the day of the murder?"

"Yes, sir; he had a purse, and he must have taken it with him because he didn't leave it in his room."

"What sort of a purse was it?"

"A brown leather purse, sir."

"Was it a new one?"

"Oh, no, sir; it was well worn."

"How big was it? About like mine?" Riedau took out his own pocketbook.

"No, sir; it was a little smaller. It had three pockets in it. I mended it for him once, so I know it well. I didn't have any brown thread so I mended it with yellow."

Dr. von Riedau nodded to Muller. The latter had been sitting at a little side-table writing down the questions and answers. When Riedau saw this he did not send for a clerk to do the work, for Muller preferred to attend to such matters himself as much as possible. The facts gained in the examination were impressed upon his mind while he was writing them, and he did not have to wade through pages of manuscript to get at what he needed. Now he handed his superior officer the paper.

"Thank you," said Riedau, "I'll send it out to the other police stations. I will attend to this myself. You go on with these people to see whether they can identify the corpse."

Fifteen minutes later the three stood before the body in the morgue and both the bookkeeper and his companion identified the dead man positively as Leopold Winkler.

When the identification was made, a notice was sent out to all Austrian police stations and to all pawnshops with an exact description of the stolen watch and purse.

Muller led his companions back to the commissioner's office and they made their report to Dr. von Riedau. Upon being questioned further, Pokorny stated: "I had very little to do with Winkler. We met only when he had a report to make to me or to show me his books, and we never met outside the office. The clerks who worked in the same room with him, may know him better.. I know only that he was a very reserved man and very little liked."

"Then I do not need to detain you any longer, nor to trouble you further in this affair. I thank you for coming to us so promptly. It has been of great assistance."

The bookkeeper left the station, but Mrs. Klingmayer, who was now quite reassured as to the harmlessness of the police, was asked to remain and to tell what she knew of the private life of the murdered man. Her answers to the various questions put to her proved that she knew very little about her tenant. But this much was learned from her: that he was very close with his money at times, but that again at other times he seemed to have all he wanted to spend. At such times he paid all his debts, and when he stayed home for supper, he would send her out for all sorts of expensive delicacies. These extravagant days seemed to have nothing whatever to do with Winkler's business pay day, but came at odd times.

Mrs. Klingmayer remembered two separate times when he had received a postal money order. But she did not know from whom the letters came, nor even whether they were sent from the city or from some other town. Winkler received other letters now and then, but his landlady was not of the prying kind, and she had paid very little attention to them.

He seemed to have few friends or even acquaintances. She did not know of any love affair, at least of nothing "regular." He had remained away over night two or three times during the year that he had been her tenant. This was about all that Mrs. Klingmayer could say, and she returned to her home in a cab furnished her by the kind commissioner.

About two hours later, a police attendant announced that a gentleman would like to see Dr. von Riedan on business concerning the murder in Hietzing. "Friedrich Bormann" was the name on the card.

"Ask him to step in here," said the commissioner. "And please ask Mr. Muller to join us."

The good-looking young clerk entered the office bashfully and Muller slipped in behind him, seating himself inconspicuously by the door. At a sign from the commissioner the visitor began. "I am an employee of Braun & Co. I have the desk next to Leopold Winkler, during the year that he has been with us — the year and a quarter to be exact — "

"Ah, then you know him rather well?"

"Why, yes. At least we were together all day, although I never met him outside the office."

"Then you cannot tell us much about his private life?"

"No, sir, but there was something happened on Monday, and in talking it over with Mr. Braun, he suggested that I should come to you and tell you about it. It wasn't really very important, and it doesn't seem as if it could have anything to do with this murder and robbery; still it may be of some use."

"Everything that would throw light on the dead man's life could be of use," said Dr. von Riedau. "Please tell us what it is you know."

Fritz Bormann began: "Winkler came to the office as usual on Monday morning and worked steadily at his desk. But I happened to notice that he spoiled several letters and had to rewrite them, which showed me that his thoughts were not on his work, a frequent occurrence with him. However, everything went along as usual until 11 o'clock. Then Winkler became very uneasy. He looked constantly toward the door, compared his watch with the office clock, and sprang up impatiently as the special letter carrier, who usually comes about 11 with money orders, finally appeared."

"Then he was expecting money you think?"

"It must have been so. For as the letter carrier passed him, he called out: 'Haven't you anything for me?' and as the man shook his head Winkler seemed greatly disappointed and depressed. Before he left to go to lunch, he wrote a hasty letter, which he put in his pocket.

"He came in half an hour later than the rest of us. He had often been reprimanded for his lack of punctuality, but it seemed to do no good. He was almost always late. Monday was no exception, although he was later than usual that day."

"And what sort of a mood was he in when he came back?"

"He was irritable and depressed. He seemed to be awaiting a message which did not come. His excitement hindered him from working, he scarcely did anything the entire afternoon. Finally at five o'clock a messenger boy came with a letter for him. I saw that Winkler turned pale as he took the note in his hand. It seemed to be only a few words written hastily on a card, thrust into an envelope. Winkler's teeth were set as he opened the letter. The messenger had already gone away."

"Did you notice his number?" asked Dr. von Riedau.

"No, I scarcely noticed the man at all. I was looking at Winkler, whose behaviour was so peculiar. When he read the card his face brightened. He read it through once more, then he tore both card and envelope into little bits and threw the pieces out of the open window.

"Then he evidently did not want anybody to see the contents of this note," said a voice from the corner of the room.

Fritz Bormann looked around astonished and rather doubtful at the little man who had risen from his chair and now came forward. Without waiting for an answer from the clerk, the other continued: "Did Winkler have money sent him frequently?"

Bormann looked inquiringly at the commissioner, who replied with a smile: "You may answer. Answer anything that Mr. Muller has to ask of you, as he is in charge of this case."

"As far as I can remember, it happened three times," was Bormann's answer.

"How close together?"

"Why — about once in every three or four months, I think."

"That looks almost like a regular income," exclaimed Riedau. His eyes met Muller's, which were lit up in sudden fire. "Well, what are you thinking of?" asked the commissioner.

"A woman," answered Muller; and continued more as if thinking aloud than as if addressing the others: "Winkler was a good-looking man. Might he not have had a rich love somewhere? Might not the money have come from her, the money that was found in his pocket?" Muller's voice trailed off into indistinctness at the last words, and the fire died out of his eyes. Then he laughed aloud.

The commissioner smiled also, a good-natured smile, such as one would give to a child who has been over-eager. "It doesn't matter to us where the money came from. All that matters here is where the bullet came from — the bullet which prevented his enjoying this money. And it is of more interest to us to find out who robbed him of his life and his property, rather than the source from which this property came."

The commissioner's tone was friendly, but Muller's face flushed red, and his, head dropped. Riedau turned to Bormann and continued: "And because it is of no interest to us where his money came from — for it can have nothing whatever to do with his murder and the subsequent robbery

— therefore what you noticed of his behaviour cannot be of any importance or bearing in the case in any way. Unless, indeed, you should find out anything more. But we appreciate the thoughtfulness of yourself and your employer and your readiness to help us."

Bormann rose to leave, but the commissioner put out a hand to stop him. "A few moments more, please; you may know of something else that will be of assistance to us. We have heard that Winkler boasted of his belongings-did he talk about his private affairs in any way?"

"No, sir, I do not think he did."

"You say that he destroyed the note at once, evidently realising that no one must see it — this note may have been a promise for the money which had not yet come. Did he, however, tell any one later that he expected a certain sum? Do you think he would have been likely to tell any one?"

"No, I do not think that he would tell any one. He never mentioned to any of us that he had received money, or even that he expected to receive it. None of us knew what outside resources he might have, or whence they came. If it had not been that the money was paid him by the carrier in the office two or three times — so, that we could see it — we would none of us have known of this income, except for the fact that he was freer in spending after the money came. He would dine at expensive restaurants, and this fact he would mention to us, whereas at other times he would go to the cheap cafe."

"Do you know anything about the people he was acquainted with outside the office?"

"No, sir. I seldom met him outside of the office. One evening it did happen that I saw him at Ronacher's. He was there with a lady — that is, a so-called 'lady '-and it must have been one of the times that he had money, for they were enjoying an expensive supper. At other times, some of the other clerks met him at various resorts, always with the same sort of woman. But not always with the same woman, for they were different in appearance."

"He was never seen anywhere with other men?"

"No, sir; at least not by any of us."

"He was not liked in the office?"

"No." Bormann's answer was sharp.

"For what reason?"

"I don't know; we just didn't like him. We had very little to do with him at first because of this, and soon we noticed that he seemed just as anxious to avoid us as we were to avoid him."

The commissioner rose and Bormann followed his example. "I am very sorry, sir, if I have taken up your time to no purpose," said the latter modestly, as he took up his hat.

"I am not so sure that what you have said may not be of great value to us," said a voice behind them. Muller stood there, looking at Riedau with a glance almost of defiance. His eyes were again lit up with the strange fire that shone in them when he was on the trail. The commissioner shrugged his shoulders, bowed to the departing visitor, and then turned without an answer to some documents on his desk. There was silence in the room for a few moments. Finally a gentle voice came from Muller's corner again: "Dr. von Riedau?"

The commissioner raised his head and looked around. "Oh, are you still there?" he asked with a drawl.

Muller knew what this drawl meant. It was the manner adopted by the amiable commissioner when he was in a mood which was not amiable. And Muller knew also the cause of the mood. It was his own last remark, the words he addressed to Bormann. Muller himself recognised the fact that this remark was out of place, that it was almost an impertinence, because it was in direct contradiction to a statement made a few moments before by his superior officer. Also he realised that his remark had been quite unnecessary, because it was a matter of indifference to the young man, who was only obeying his employer's orders in reporting what he had seen, whether his report was of value or not. Muller had simply uttered aloud the thought that came into his mind, a habit of his which years of official training had not yet succeeded in breaking. It was annoying to himself sometimes, for these half-formed thoughts were mere instinct — they were the workings of his own genius that made him catch a suspicion of the truth long before his conscious mind could reason it out or appreciate its value. But that sort of thing was not popular in official police life.

"Well," asked the commissioner, as Muller did not continue, "your tongue is not usually so slow — as you have proved just a few moments back — what were you going to say now?"

"I was about to ask your pardon for my interruption. It was unnecessary, I should not have said it."

"Well, I realise that you know better yourself," said Riedau, now quite friendly again, "and now what else have you to say? Do you really think that what the young man has just told us is of any value at all for this case?"

"It seems to me as if it might be of value to us."

"Oh, it seems to you, eh? Your imagination is working overtime again, Muller," said the commissioner with a laugh. But the laugh turned to seriousness as he realised how many times Muller's imagination had helped the clumsy official mind to its proudest triumphs. The commissioner was an intelligent man, as far as his lights went, and he was a good-hearted man. He rose from his chair and walked over to where the detective stood. "You needn't look so embarrassed, Muller," he said. "There is no cause for you to feel bad about it. And — I am quite willing to admit that my remark just now was unnecessary. You may give your imagination full rein, we can trust to your intelligence and your devotion to duty to keep it from unnecessary flights. So curbed, I know it will be of as much assistance to us this time as it always has been."

Muller's quiet face lit up, and his eyes shone in a happiness that made him appear ten years younger. That was one of the strange things about Joseph Muller. This genius in his profession was in all other ways a man of such simplicity of heart and bearing, that the slightest word of approval from one of the officials for whom he worked could make him as happy as praise from the teacher will make a schoolboy. The moments when he was in command of any difficult case, when these same superiors would wait for a word from him, when high officials would take his orders or would be obliged to acknowledge that without him they were helpless, these moments were forgotten as soon as the problem was solved and Muller became again the simple subordinate and the obscure member of the Imperial police force.

When Muller left the commissioner's room

and walked through the outer office, one of the clerks looked after him and whispered to his companion: "Do you think he's found the Hietzing murderer yet?" The other answered: "I don't think so, but he looks as if he had found a clue. He'll find him sooner or later. He always does."

Muller did not hear these words, although they also would have pleased him. He walked slowly down the stairs murmuring to himself: "I think I was right just the same. We are following a false trail."

CHAPTER V. BY A THREAD

It was on Monday, the 27th of September, that Leopold Winkler was murdered and robbed, and early on Tuesday, the 28th, his body was found. That day the evening papers printed the report of the murder and the description of the dead man, and on Wednesday, the 29th, Mrs. Klingmayer read the news and went to see Winkler's employer. By noon of that day the body was identified and a description of the stolen purse and watch telegraphed to police headquarters in various cities. A few hours later, these police stations had sent out notices by messenger to all pawnshops and dealers in second-hand clothing, and now the machinery of the law sat waiting for some news of an attempt on the part of the robber-and-murderer to get rid of his plunder.

On this same Wednesday, about the twilight hour, David Goldstamm, dealer in second-hand clothing, stood before the door of his shop in a side street of the old Hungarian city of Pressburg and watched his assistant take down the clothes which were hanging outside and carry them into the store. The old man's eyes glanced carelessly up and down the street and caught sight of a man who turned the corner and came hurrying towards him. This man was a very seedy-looking individual. An old faded overcoat hung about his thin figure, and a torn and dusty hat fell over his left eye. He seemed also to be much the worse for liquor and very wobbly on his feet. And yet he seemed anxious to hurry onward in spite of the unevenness of his walk.

Then he slowed up suddenly, glanced across the street to Goldstamm's store, and crossed over.

"Have you any boots for me?" he asked, sticking out his right foot that the dealer might see whether he had anything the requisite size.

"I think there's something there," answered the old man in his usual businesslike tone, leading the way into the store.

The stranger followed. Goldstamm lit the one light in the little place and groped about in an untidy heap of shoes of all kinds and sizes until he found several pairs that he thought might fit. These he brought out and put them in front of his customer. But in spite of his bleary eyes, the man caught sight of some patches on the uppers of one pair, and pushed them away from him.

"Give me something better than that. I can pay for it. I don't have to wear patched shoes," he grunted.

Goldstamm didn't like the looks of the man, but he felt that he had better be careful and not make him angry. "Have patience, sir, I'll find you something better," he said gently, tossing the heap about again, but now keeping his face turned towards his customer.

"I want a coat also and a warm pair of trousers," said the stranger in a rough voice. He bent down to loosen the shabby boot from his right foot, and as he did so something fell out of the pocket of his coat. An unconscious motion of his own raised foot struck this small object and tossed it into the middle of the heap of shoes close by Goldstamm's hand. The old man reached out after it and caught it. It was just an ordinary brown leather pocketbook, of medium size, old and shabby, like a thousand others. But the eyes of the little old man widened as if in terror, his face turned pale and his hands trembled. For he had seen, hanging from one side of this worn brown leather pocketbook, the end of a yellow thread, the loosened end of the thread with which one side of the purse was mended. The thread told David Goldstamm who it was that had come into his shop.

He regained his control with a desperate effort of the will. It took him but a few seconds to do so, and, thanks to his partial intoxication, the customer had not noticed the shopkeeper's start of alarm. But he appeared anxious and impatient to regain possession of his purse.

"Haven't you found it yet?" he exclaimed.

Goldstamm hastened to give it back. The tramp put the purse in his pocket with a sigh of relief. Goldstamm had regained his calm and his mind was working eagerly. He put several pairs of shoes before his customer, with the remark: "You must try them on. We'll find something to suit you. And meanwhile I will bring in several pairs of trousers from those outside. I have some fine coats to show you too."

Goldstamm went out to the door, almost colliding there with his assistant who was coming in with his arm full of garments. The old man motioned to the boy, who retreated until they were both hidden from the view of the man within the store.

"Give me those blue trousers there," said Goldstamm in a loud voice. Then in a whisper he said to the boy: "Run to the police station. The man with the watch and the purse is in there."

The boy understood and set off at once at a fast pace, while the old man returned to his store with a heavy heart. He wondered whether he would be able to keep the murderer there until the police could come. And he also wondered what it might cost him, an old and feeble man, who would be as a weak reed in the hands of the strong tramp in there. But he knew it was his duty to do whatever he could to help in the arrest of one who had just taken the life of a fellow creature. The realisation of this gave the old man strength and calmness.

"A nice sort of an eye for size you have," cried the tramp as the old man came up to him. "I suppose you've brought me in a boy's suit? What do you take me for? Any girl could go to a ball in the shoes you brought me to try on here."

"Are they so much too small?" asked the

dealer in an innocent tone. "Well, there's plenty more there. And perhaps you had better be trying on this suit behind the curtain here while I'm hunting up the shoes."

This suggestion seemed to please the stranger, as he was evidently in a hurry. He passed in behind the curtain and began to undress. Goldstamm's keen eyes watched him through a crack. There was not much to be seen except that the tramp seemed anxious to keep his overcoat within reach of his hand. He had carefully put the purse in one of its pockets.

"We'll get the things all together pretty soon," said the dealer. "I've found a pair of boots here, fine boots of good quality, and sure to fit."

"Stop your talk," growled the other, "and come here and help me so that I can get away."

Goldstamm came forward, and though his heart was very heavy within him, he aided this man, this man about whom so many hundreds were now thinking in terror, as calmly as he had aided his other poor but honest customers.

With hands that did not tremble, the dealer busied himself about his customer, listening all the while to sounds in the street in the hope that his tete-e-tete with the murderer would soon be over. But in spite of all his natural anxiety, the old man's sharp eyes took cognizance of various things, one of which was that the man whom he was helping to dress in his new clothes did not have the watch which was described in the police notice. This fact, however, did not make the old man's heart any lighter, for the purse mended with yellow thread was too clearly the one stolen from the murdered man found in the quiet street in Hietzing.

"What's the matter with you, you're so slow? I can get along better myself," growled the tramp, pushing the old man away from him. Goldstamm had really begun to tremble now in spite of his control, in the fear that the man would get away from him before the police came.

The tramp was already dressed in the new suit, into a pocket of which he put the old purse.

"There, now the boots and then we're finished," said the dealer with an attempt at a smile. In his heart he prayed that the pair he now held in his hand might not fit, that he might gain a few minutes more. But the shoes did fit. A little pushing and stamping and the man was ready to leave the store. He was evidently in a hurry, for he paid what was asked without any attempt to bargain. Had Goldstamm not known whom he had before him now, he would have been very much astonished at this, and might perhaps have been sorry that he had not named a higher sum. But under the circumstances he understood only too well the man's desire to get away, and would much rather have had some talk as to the payment, anything that would keep his customer a little longer in his store.

"There, now we're ready. I'll pack up your old things for you. Or perhaps we can make a deal for them. I pay the highest prices in the city," said Goldstamm, with an apparent eagerness which he hoped would deceive the customer.

But the man had already turned towards the door, and called hack over his shoulder: "You can keep the old things, I don't want them."

As he spoke he opened the door of the store and stood face to face with a policeman holding a revolver. He turned, with a curse, back into the room, but the dealer was nowhere to be seen. David Goldstamm had done his duty to the public, in spite of his fear. Now, seeing that the police had arrived, he could think of his duty to his family. This duty was plainly to save his own life, and when the tramp turned again to look for him, he had disappeared out of the back door.

"Not a move or I will shoot," cried the policeman, and now two others appeared behind him, and came into the store. But the tramp made no attempt to escape. He stood pale and trembling while they put the handcuffs on him, and let them take him away without any resistance. He was put on the evening express for Vienna, and taken to Police Headquarters in that city. He made no protest nor any attempt to escape, but he refused to utter a word on the entire journey.

CHAPTER VI. ALMOST CONVICTED

The evening was already far gone when Muller entered Riedau's office.

"You're in time, the man isn't here yet. The train is evidently late," said the commissioner. "We're working this case off quickly. We will have the murderer here in half an hour at the latest. He did not have much time to enjoy the stolen property. He was here in Vienna this morning, and was arrested in Pressburg this afternoon. Here is the telegram, read it."

Dr. von Riedau handed Muller the message. The commissioner was evidently pleased and excited. The telegram read as follows: "Man arrested here in possession of described purse containing four ten gulden notes and four guldens in silver. Arrested in store of second-hand clothes dealer Goldstamm. Will arrive this evening in Vienna under guard."

The message was signed by the Chief of the Pressburg police.

Muller laid the paper on the desk without a word. There was a watch on this desk already; it was a heavy gold watch, unusually thick, with the initials L. W. on the cover. Just as Muller laid down the telegram, a door outside was opened and the commissioner covered the watch hastily. There was a loud knock at his own door and an attendant entered to announce that the party from Pressburg had arrived He was followed by one of the Pressburg police force, who brought the official report.

"Did you have any difficulty with him?" asked the commissioner.

"Oh, no, sir; it was a very easy job. He made no resistance at all, and he seems to be quite sober now. But he hasn't said a word since we arrested him."

Then followed the detailed report of the arrest, and the delivery of the described pocketbook to the commissioner.

"Is that all?" asked Dr. von Riedau.

"Yes, sir."

"Then you may go home now, we will take charge of the man."

The policeman bowed and left the room. A few moments later the tramp was brought in, guarded by two armed roundsmen. His guards remained at the door, while the prisoner himself walked forward to the middle of the room. Commissioner von Riedau sat at his desk, his clerk beside him ready to take down the evidence. Muller sat near a window with a paper on his lap, looking the least interested of anybody in the proceedings.

For a moment there was complete silence in the room, which was broken in a rather unusual manner. A deep voice, more like a growl, although it had a queer strain of comic good-nature in it, began the proceedings with the remark: "Well now, say, what do you want of me, anyway?"

The commissioner looked at the man in astonishment, then turned aside that the prisoner might not notice his smile. But he might have spared himself the trouble, for Muller, the clerk, and the two policemen at the door were all on a broad grin.

Then the commissioner pulled himself together again, and began with his usual official gravity: "It is I who ask questions here. Is it possible that you do not know this? You look to me as if you had had experience in police courts before." The commissioner gazed at the prisoner with eyes that were not altogether friendly. The tramp seemed to feel this, and his own eyes dropped, while the good-natured impertinence in his bearing disappeared. It was evidently the last remains of his intoxication. He was now quite sober.

"What is your name?" asked the commissioner.

"Johann Knoll."

"Where were you born?"

"Near Brunn."

"Your age?"

"I'm — I'll be forty next Christmas."

"Your religion?"

"Well, you can see I'm no Jew, can't you?"

"You will please answer my questions in a proper manner. This impertinence will not make things easier for you."

"All right, sir," said the tramp humbly. "I am a Catholic."

"You have been in prison before?" This was scarcely a question.

"No, sir," said Knoll firmly.

"What is your business?"

"I don't know what to say, sir," answered Knoll, shrugging his shoulders. "I've done a lot of things in my life. I'm a cattle drover and a lumber man, and I — "

"Did you learn any trade?"

"No, sir, I never learned anything."

"Do you mean to tell me that without having learned any trade you've gotten through life thus far honestly?"

"Oh, I've worked hard enough — I've worked good and hard sometimes."

"The last few days particularly, eh?"

"Why, no, sir, not these last days — I was drover on a transport of pigs; we brought 'em down from Hungary, 200 of 'em, to the slaughter house here."

"When was that?"

"That was — that was Monday."

"This last Monday?"

"Yes, sir.

"And then you went to Hietzing?"

"Yes, sir, that's right."

"Why did you go to Hietzing?"

"Why, see here, sir, if I had gone to Ottak-ring, then I suppose you would have asked why did I go to Ottakring. I just went to Hietzing. A fellow has to go somewhere. You don't stay in the same spot all the time, do you?"

Again the commissioner turned his head and another smile went through the room. This Hietz-ing murderer had a sense of humour.

"Well, then, we'll go to Hietzing again, in our minds at least," said the commissioner, turning back to Knoll when he had controlled his merri-ment. "You went there on Monday, then — and the day was coming to an end. What did you do when you reached Hietzing?"

"I looked about for a place to sleep."

"Where did you look for a place to sleep?"

"Why, in Hietzing."

"That is not definite enough."

"Well, in a garden."

"You were trespassing, you mean?"

"Why, yes, sir. There wasn't anybody that seemed to want to invite me to dinner or to give me a place to sleep. I just had to look out for myself."

"You evidently know how to look out for yourself at the cost of others, a heavy cost." The commissioner's easy tone had changed to sternness. Knoll felt this, and a sharp gleam shot out from his dull little eyes, while the tone of his voice was gruff and impertinent again as he asked: "What do you mean by that?"

"You know well enough. You had better not waste any more time, but tell us at once how you came into possession of this purse."

"It's my purse," Knoll answered with calm impertinence. "I got it the way most people get it. I bought it."

"This purse?" the commissioner emphasised both words distinctly.

"This purse — yes," answered the tramp with a perfect imitation of Riedau's voice. "Why shouldn't I have bought this purse just like any other?"

"Because you stole this purse from the man whom you — murdered," was the commissioner's reply.

There was another moment of dead silence in the room. The commissioner and Muller watched intently for any change of expression in the face of the man who had just had such an accusation hurled at him. Even the clerk and the two policemen at the door were interested to see what would happen.

Knoll's calm impertinence vanished, a deadly pallor spread over his face, and he seemed frozen to stone. He attempted to speak, but was not able to control his voice. His hands were clenched and tremors shook his gaunt but strong-muscled frame.

"When did I murder anybody?" he gasped finally in a hoarse croak. "You'll have to prove it to me that I am a murderer."

"That is easily proved. Here is one of the proofs," said Riedan coldly, pointing to the purse. "The purse and the watch of the murdered man are fatal witnesses against you."

"The watch? I haven't any watch. Where should I get a watch?"

"You didn't have one until Monday, possibly; I can believe that. But you were in possession of a watch between the evening of Monday, the 27th, and the morning of Wednesday, the 29th."

Knoll's eyes dropped again and he did not trust himself to speak.

"Well, you do not deny this statement?"

"No, I can't," said Knoll, still trying to control his voice. "You must have the watch yourself now, or else you wouldn't be so certain about it."

"Ah, you see, I thought you'd had experience with police courts before," said the commissioner amiably. "Of course I have the watch already. The man whom you sold it to this morning knew by three o'clock this afternoon where this watch came from. He brought it here at once and gave us your description. A very exact description. The man will be brought here to identify you tomorrow. We must send for him anyway, to return his money to him. He paid you fifty-two gulden for the watch. And how much money was in the purse that you took from the murdered man?"

"Three gulden eighty-five."

"That was a very small sum for which to commit a murder."

Knoll groaned and bit his lips until they bled.

Commissioner von Riedau raised the paper that covered the watch and continued: "You presumably recognised that the chain on which this watch hung was valueless, also that it could easily be recognised. Did you throw it away, or have you it still?"

"I threw it in the river."

"That will not make any difference. We do

not need the chain, we have quite enough evidence without it. The purse, for instance: you thought, I suppose, that it was just a purse like a thousand others, but it is not. This purse is absolutely individual and easily recognised, because it is mended in one spot with yellow thread. The thread has become loosened and hangs down in a very noticeable manner. It was this yellow thread on the purse, which he happened to see by chance, that showed the dealer Goldstamm who it was that had entered his store."

Knoll stood quite silent, staring at the floor. Drops of perspiration stood out on his forehead, some of them rolling like tears down his cheek.

The commissioner rose from his seat and walked slowly to where the prisoner stood. He laid one hand on the man's shoulder and said in a voice that was quite gentle and kind again: "Johann Knoll, do not waste your time, or ours, in thinking up useless lies. You are almost convicted of this crime now. You have already acknowledged so much, that there is but little more for you to say. If you make an open confession, it will be greatly to your advantage."

Again the room was quiet while the others waited for what would happen. For a moment the tramp stood silent, with the commissioner's right hand resting on his shoulder. Then there was a sudden movement, a struggle and a shout, and the two policemen had overpowered the prisoner and held him firmly. Muller rose quickly and sprang to his chief's side. Riedau had not even changed colour, and he said calmly: "Oh, never mind, Muller; sit down again. The man had handcuffs on and he is quite quiet now. I think he has sense enough to see that he is only harming himself by his violence."

The commissioner returned to his desk and Muller went back to his chair by the window. The prisoner was quiet again, although his face wore a dark flush and the veins on throat and forehead were swollen thick. He trembled noticeably and the heavy drops besprinkled his brow.

"I — I have something to say, sir," he began, "but first I want to beg your pardon — "

"Oh, never mind that. I am not angry when a man is fighting for his life, even if he doesn't choose quite the right way," answered the commissioner calmly, playing with a lead pencil.

Knoll's expression was defiant now. He laughed harshly and began again: "What I'm tellin' you now is the truth whether you believe it or not. I didn't kill the man. I took the watch and purse from him. I thought he was drunk. If he was killed, I didn't do it."

"He was killed by a shot."

"A shot? Why, yes, I heard a shot, but I didn't think any more about it, I didn't think there was anythin' doing, I thought somebody was shootin' a cat, or else-"

"Oh, don't bother to invent things. It was a man who was shot at, the man whom you robbed. But go on, go on. I am anxious to hear what you will tell me."

Knoll's hands, clenched to fists and his eyes glowed in hate and defiance. Then he dropped them to the floor again and began to talk slowly in a monotonous tone that sounded as if he were repeating a lesson. His manner was rather unfortunate and did not tend to induce belief in the truth of his story. The gist of what he said was as follows:

He had reached Hietzing on Monday evening about 8 o'clock. He was thirsty, as usual, and had about two gulden in his possession, his wages for the last day's work. He turned into a tavern in Hietzing and ate and drank until his money was all gone, and he had not even enough left to pay for a night's lodging. But Knoll was not worried about that. He was accustomed to sleeping out of doors, and as this was a particularly fine evening, there was nothing in the prospect to alarm him. He set about finding a suitable place where he would not be disturbed by the guardians of the law. His search led him by chance into a newly opened street. This suited him exactly. The fences were easy to climb, and there were several little summer houses in sight which made much more agreeable lodgings than the ground under a bush. And above all, the street was so quiet and deserted that he knew it was just the place for him. He had never been in the street before, and did not know its name. He passed the four houses at the end of the street — he was on the left sidewalk — and then he came to two fenced-in building lots. These interested him. He was very agile, raised himself up on the fences easily and took stock of the situation. One of the lots did not appeal to him particularly, but the second one did. It bordered on a large garden, in the middle of which he could see a little house of some kind. It was after sunset but he could see things quite plainly yet for the air was clear and the moon was just rising. He saw also that in the vacant lot adjoining the garden, a lot which appeared to have been a garden itself once, there was a sort of shed. It looked very much damaged but appeared to offer shelter sufficient for a fine night.

The shed stood on a little raise of the ground near the high iron fence that protected the large garden. Knoll decided that the shed would make a good place to spend the night. He climbed the fence easily and walked across the lot. When he was just settling himself for his nap, he heard the clock on a near-by church strike nine. The various drinks he had had for supper put him in a mood that would not allow him to get to sleep at once. The bench in the old shed was decidedly rickety and very uncomfortable, and as he was tossing about to find a good position, a thought came into his mind which he acknowledged was not a commendable one. It occurred to him that if he pursued his investigations in the neighbourhood a little further, he might be able to pick up something that would be of advantage to him on his wanderings. His eyes and his thoughts were directed towards the handsome house which he could see beyond the trees of the old garden.

The moon was now well up in the sky and it shone brightly on the mansard roof of the fine old mansion. The windows of the long wing which stretched out towards the garden glistened in the moonbeams, and the light coloured wall of the house made a bright background for the dark mask of trees waving gently in the night breeze. Knoll's little shed was sufficiently raised on its hillock for him to have a good view of the garden. There was no door to the shed and he could see the neighbouring property clearly from where he lay on his bench. While he lay there watching, he saw a woman walking through the garden. He could see her only when she passed back of or between the lower shrubs and bushes. As far as he could see, she came from the main building and was walking towards a pretty little house which lay in the centre of the garden. Knoll had imagined this house to be the gardener's dwelling and as it lay quite dark he supposed the inmates were either asleep or out for the evening. It had been this house which he was intending to honour by a visit. But seeing the woman walking towards it, he decided it would not be safe to carry out his plan just yet awhile.

A few moments later he was certain that this last decision had been a wise one, for he saw a man come from the main building and walk along the path the woman had taken. "No, nothing doing there," thought Knoll, and concluded he had better go to sleep. He could not remember just how long he may have dozed but it seemed to him that during that time he had heard a shot. It did not interest him much. He supposed some one was shooting at a thieving cat or at some small night animal. He did not even remember whether he had been really sound asleep, before he was aroused by the breaking down of the bench on which he lay. The noise of it more than the shock of the short fall, awoke him and he sprang tip in alarm and listened intently to hear whether any one had been attracted by it. His first glance was towards the building behind the garden. There was no sound nor no light in the garden house but there was a light in the main building. While the tramp was wondering what hour it might be, the church clock answered him by ten loud strokes.

His head was already aching from the wine and he did not feel comfortable in the drafty old building. He came out from it, crept along to the spot where he had climbed the fence before, and after listening carefully and hearing nothing on either side, he climbed back to the road. The Street lay silent and empty, which was just what he was hoping for. He held carefully to the shadow thrown by the high board fence over which he had climbed until he came to its end. Then he remembered that he hadn't done anything wrong and stepped out boldly into the moonlight. The moon was well up now and the street was almost as light as day. Knoll was attracted by the queer shadows thrown by a big elder tree, waving its long branches in the wind. As he came nearer he saw that part of the shadow was no shadow at all but was the body of a man lying in the street near the bush. "I thought sure he was drunk" was the way Knoll described it. "I've been like that myself often until somebody came along and found me."

When he came to this spot in his story, he halted and drew a long breath. Commissioner von Riedau had begun to make some figures on the paper in front of him, then changed the lines until the head of a pretty woman in a fur hat took shape under his fingers.

"Well, go on," he said, looking with interest at his drawing and improving it with several quick strokes.

Johann Knoll continued:

"Then the devil came over me and I thought I better take this good opportunity — well — I did. The man was lying on his back and I saw a watch chain on his dark vest. I bent over him and took his watch and chain. Then I felt around in his pocket and found his purse. And then — well then I felt sorry for him lying out in the open road like that, and I thought I'd lift him up and put him somewhere where he could sleep it off more convenient. But I didn't see there was a little ditch there and I stumbled over it and dropped him. 'It's a good thing he's so drunk that even this don't wake him up,' I thought, and ran off. Then I thought I heard something moving and I was scared stiff, but there was nothing in the street at all. I thought I had better take to the fields though and I crossed through some corn and then out onto another street. Finally I walked into the city, stayed there till this morning, sold the watch, then went to Pressburg."

"So that was the way it was," said the commissioner, pushing his drawing away from him and motioning to the policemen at the door. "You may take this man away now," he added in a voice of cool indifference, without looking at the prisoner.

Knoll's head drooped and he walked out quietly between his two guards. The clock on the office wall struck eleven.

"Dear me! what a lot of time the man wasted," said the commissioner, putting the report of the proceedings, the watch and the purse in a drawer of his desk. "When anybody has been almost convicted of a crime, it's really quite unnecessary to invent such a long story."

A few minutes later, the room was empty and Muller, as the last of the group, walked slowly down the stairs. He was in such a brown study that he scarcely heard the commissioner's friendly "goodnight," nor did he notice that he was walking down the quiet street under a star-gilded sky. "Almost convicted — almost. Almost?" Muller's lips murmured while his head was full of a chaotic rush of thought, dim pictures that came and went, something that seemed to be on the point of bringing light into the darkness, then vanishing again. "Almost — but not quite. There is something here I must find out first. What is it? I must know — "

CHAPTER VII. THE FACE AT THE GATE

The second examination of the prisoner brought nothing new. Johann Knoll refused to speak at all, or else simply repeated what he had said before. This second examination took place early the next morning, but Muller was not present. He was taking a walk in Hietzing.

When they took Johann Knoll in the police wagon to the City Prison, Muller was just sauntering slowly through the street where the murder had been committed. And as the door of the cell shut clangingly behind the man whose face was distorted in impotent rage and despair, Joseph Muller was standing in deep thought before the broken willow twig, which now hung brown and dry across the planks of the fence. He looked at it for a long time. That is, he seemed to be looking at it, but in reality his eyes were looking out and beyond the willow twig, out into the unknown, where the unknown murderer was still at large. Leopold Winkler's body had already been committed to the earth. How long will it be before his death is avenged? Or perhaps how long may it even be before it is discovered from what motive this murder was committed. Was it a murder for robbery, or a murder for personal revenge perhaps? Were the two crimes committed here by one and the same person, or were there two people concerned? And if two, did they work as accomplices? Or is it possible that Knoll's story was true? Did he really only rob the body, not realising that it was a dead man and not merely an intoxicated sleeper as he had supposed? These and many more thoughts rushed tumultuously through Muller's brain until he sighed despairingly under the pressure. Then he smiled in amusement at the wish that had crossed his brain, the wish that this case might seem as simple to him as it apparently did to the commissioner. It would certainly have saved him a lot of work and trouble if he could believe the obvious as most people did. What was this devil that rode him and spurred him on to delve into the hidden facts concerning matters that seemed so simple on the surface? The devil that spurred him on to understand that there always was some hidden side to every case? Then the sigh and the smile passed, and Muller raised his head in one of the rare moments of pride in his own gifts that this shy unassuming little man ever allowed himself. This was the work that he was intended by Providence to do or he wouldn't have been fitted for it, and it was work for the common good, for the public safety. Thinking back over the troubles of his early youth, Muller's heart rejoiced and he was glad in his own genius. Then the moment of unwonted elation passed and he bent his mind again to the problem before him.

He sauntered slowly through the quiet street in the direction of the four houses. To reach them he passed the fence that enclosed this end of the Thorne property. Muller had already known, for the last twenty-four hours at least, that the owner of the fine old estate was an artist by the name of Herbert Thorne. His own landlady had informed him of this. He himself was new to the neighbourhood, having moved out there recently, and he had verified her statements by the city directory. As he was now passing the Thorne property, in his slow, sauntering walk, he had just come within a dozen paces of the little wooden gate in the fence when this gate opened. Muller's naturally soft tread was made still more noiseless by the fact that he wore wide soft shoes. Years before he had acquired a bad case of chilblains, in fact had been in imminent danger of having his feet frozen by standing for five hours in the snow in front of a house, to intercept several aristocratic gentlemen who sooner or later would be obliged to leave that house. The police had long suspected the existence of this high-class gambling den; but it was not until they had put Muller in charge of the case, that there were any results attained. The arrests were made at the risk of permanent injury to the celebrated detective. Since then, Muller's step was more noiseless than usual, and now the woman who opened the gate and peered out cautiously did not hear his approach nor did she see him standing in the shadow of the fence. She looked towards the other end of the street, then turned and spoke to somebody behind her. "There's nobody coming from that direction," he said. Then she turned her head the other way and saw Muller. She looked at him for a moment and slammed the gate shut, disappearing behind it. Muller heard the lock click and heard the beat of running feet hastening rapidly over the gravel path through the garden.

The detective stood immediately in front of the gate, shaking his head. "What was the matter with the woman? What was it that she wanted to see or do in the street? Why should she run away when she saw me?" These were his thoughts. But he didn't waste time in merely thinking. Muller never did. Action followed thought with him very quickly. He saw a knot-hole in the fence just beside the gate and he applied his eyes to this knot-hole. And through the knot-hole he saw something that interested and surprised him.

The woman whose face had appeared so suddenly at the gate, and disappeared still more suddenly, was the same woman whom he had seen bidding farewell to Mr. Thorne and his wife on the Tuesday morning previous, the woman whom he took to be the housekeeper. The old butler stood beside her. It was undoubtedly the same man, although he had worn a livery then and was now dressed in a comfortable old house coat. He stood beside the woman, shaking his head and asking her just the questions that Muller was asking himself at the moment.

"Why, what is the matter with you, Mrs. Bernaner? You're so nervous since yesterday. Are you ill? Everything seems to frighten you? Why did you run away from that gate so suddenly? I thought you wanted me to show you the place?"

Mrs. Bernauer raised her head and Muller saw that her face looked pale and haggard and that her eyes shone with an uneasy feverish light. She did not answer the old man's questions, but made a gesture of farewell and then turned and walked slowly towards the house. She realised, apparently, and feared, perhaps, that the man who was passing the gate might have, noticed her sudden change of demeanour and that he was listening to what she might say. She did not think of the knot-hole in the board fence, or she might have been more careful in hiding her distraught face from possible observers.

Muller stood watching through this knot-hole for some little time. He took a careful observation of the garden, and from his point of vantage he could easily see the little house which was apparently the dwelling of the gardener, as well as the mansard roof of the main building. There was considerable distance between the two houses. The detective decided that it might interest him to know something more about this garden, this house and the people who lived there. And when Muller made such a decision it was usually not very long before he carried it out.

The other street, upon which the main front of the mansard house opened, contained a few isolated dwellings surrounded by gardens and a number of newly built apartment houses. On the ground floor of these latter houses were a number of stores and immediately opposite the Thorne mansion was a little cafe. This suited Muller exactly, for he had been there before and he remembered that from one of the windows there was an excellent view of the gate and the front entrance of the mansion opposite. It was a very modest little cafe, but there was a fairly good wine to be had there and the detective made it an excuse to sit down by the window, as if enjoying his bottle while admiring the changing colours of the foliage in the gardens opposite.

Another rather good chance, he discovered, was the fact that the landlord belonged to the talkative sort, and believed that the refreshments he had to sell were rendered doubly agreeable when spiced by conversation. In this case the good man was not mistaken. It was scarcely ten o'clock in the forenoon and there were very few people in the cafe. The landlord was quite at leisure to devote himself to this stranger in the window seat, whom he did not remember to have seen before, and who was therefore doubly interesting to him. Several subjects of conversation usual in such cases, such as politics and the weather, seemed to arouse no particular enthusiasm in his patron's manner. Finally the portly landlord decided that he would touch upon the theme which was still absorbing all Hietzing.

"Oh, by the way, sir, do you know that you are in the immediate vicinity of the place where the murder of Monday evening was committed? People are still talking about it around here. And

I see by the papers that the murderer was arrested in Pressburg yesterday and brought to Vienna last night."

"Indeed, is that so? I haven't seen a paper to-day," replied Muller, awakening from his apparent indifference.

The landlord was flattered by the success of the new subject, and stood ready to unloose the floodgates of his eloquence. His customer sat up and asked the question for which the landlord was waiting.

"So it was around here that the man was shot?"

"Yes. His name was Leopold Winkler, that was in the papers to-day too. You see that pretty house opposite? Well, right behind this house is the garden that belongs to it and back of that, an old garden which has been neglected for some time. It was at the end of this garden where it touches the other street, that they found the man under a big elder-tree, early Tuesday morning, day before yesterday."

"Oh, indeed!" said. Muller, greatly interested, as if this was the first he had heard of it. The landlord took a deep breath and was about to begin again when his customer, who decided to keep the talkative man to a certain phase of the subject, now took command of the conversation himself.

"I should think that the people opposite, who live so near the place where the murder was committed, wouldn't be very much pleased," he said. "I shouldn't care to look out on such a spot every time I went to my window."

"There aren't any windows there," exclaimed the landlord, "for there aren't any houses there. There's only the old garden, and then the large garden and the park belonging to Mr. Thorne's house, that fine old house you see just opposite here. It's a good thing that Mr. Thorne and his wife went away before the murder became known. The lady hasn't been well for some weeks, she's very nervous and frail, and it probably would have frightened her to think that such things were happening right close to her home."

"The lady is sick? What's the matter with her?"

"Goodness knows, nerves, heart trouble, something like that. The things these fine ladies are always having. But she wasn't always that way, not until about a year ago. She was fresh and blooming and very pretty to look at before that."

"She is a young lady then?"

"Yes, indeed, sir; she's very young still and very pretty. It makes you feel sorry to see her so miserable, and you feel sorry for her husband. Now there's a young couple with everything in the world to make them happy and so fond of each other, and the poor little lady has to be so sick."

"They are very happy, you say?" asked Muller carelessly. He had no particular set purpose in following up this inquiry, none but his usual understanding of the fact that a man in his business can never amass too much knowledge, and that it will sometimes happen that a chance bit of information comes in very handy.

The landlord was pleased at the encouragement and continued: "Indeed they are very happy. They've only been married two years. The lady comes from a distance, from Graz. Her father is an army officer I believe, and I don't think she was over-rich. But she's a very sweet-looking lady and her rich husband is very fond of her, any one can see that."

"You said just now that they had gone away, where have they gone to?"

"They've gone to Italy, sir. Mrs. Thorne was one of the few people who do not know Venice. Franz, that's the butler, sir, told me yesterday evening that he had received a telegram saying that the lady and gentleman had arrived safely and were very comfortably fixed in the Hotel Danieli. You know Danieli's?"

"Yes, I do. I also was one of the few people who did not know Venice, that is I was until two years ago. Then, however, I had the pleasure of riding over the Bridge of Mestre," answered Muller. He did not add that he was not alone at the time, but had ridden across the long bridge in company with a pale haggard-faced man who did not dare to look to the right or to the left because of the revolver which he knew was held in the detective's hand under his loose overcoat. Muller's visit to Venice, like most of his journeyings, had been one of business. This time to capture and bring home a notorious and long sought embezzler. He did not volunteer any of this information, however, but merely asked in a politely interested manner whether the landlord himself had been to Venice.

"Yes, indeed," replied the latter proudly. "I was head waiter at Baner's for two years."

"Then you must make me some Italian dishes soon," said Muller. Further conversation was interrupted by the entrance of Franz, the old butler of the house opposite.

"Excuse me, sir; I must get him his glass of wine," said the landlord, hurrying away to the bar. He returned in a moment with a small bottle and a glass and set it down on Muller's table.

"You don't mind, sir, if he sits down here?" he asked. "He usually sits here at this table because then he can see if he is needed over at the house."

"Oh, please let him come here. He has prior rights to this table undoubtedly," said the stranger politely. The old butler sat down with an embarrassed murmur, as the voluble landlord explained that the stranger had no objection. Then the boniface hurried off to attend to some newly entered customers and the detective, greatly pleased at the prospect, found himself alone with the old servant.

"You come here frequently?" he began, to open the conversation.

"Yes, sir, since my master and myself have settled down here — we travelled most of the time until several years ago — I find this place very convenient. It's a cosy little room, the wine is good and not expensive, I'm near home and yet I can see some new faces occasionally."

"I hope the faces that you see about you at home are not so unpleasant that you are glad to get away from them?" asked Muller with a smile.

The old man gave a start of alarm. "Oh, dear, no, sir," he exclaimed eagerly; "that wasn't what I meant. Indeed I'm fond of everybody in the house from our dear lady down to the poor little dog."

Here Muller gained another little bit of knowledge, the fact that the lady of the house was the favourite of her servants, or that she seemed to them even more an object of adoration than the master.

"Then you evidently have a very good place, since you seem so fond of every one."

"Indeed I have a good place, sir."

"You've had this place a long time?"

"More than twenty years. My master was only eleven years old when I took service with the family."

"Ah, indeed! then you must be a person of importance in the house if you have been there so long?"

"Well more or less I might say I am," the old man smiled and looked flattered, then added: "But the housekeeper, Mrs. Bernaner, is even more important than I am, to tell you the truth. She was nurse to our present young master, and she's been in the house ever since. When his parents died, it's some years ago now, she took entire charge of the housekeeping. She was a fine active woman then, and now the young master and mistress couldn't get along without her. They treat her as if she was one of the family."

"And she is ill also? I say also," explained Muller, "because the landlord has just been telling me that your mistress is ill."

"Yes, indeed, more's the pity! our poor dear young lady has been miserable for nearly a year now. It's a shame to see such a sweet angel as she is suffer like that and the master's quite heartbroken over it. But there's nothing the matter with Mrs. Bernaner. How did you come to think that she was sick?"

Muller did not intend to explain that the

change in the housekeeper's appearance, a change which had come about between Tuesday morning and Thursday morning, might easily have made any one think that she was ill. He gave as excuse for his question the old man's own words: "Why, I thought that she might be ill also because you said yourself that the housekeeper — what did you say her name was?"

"Bernauer, Mrs. Adele Bernauer. She was a widow when she came to take care of the master. Her husband was a sergeant of artillery."

"Well, I mean," continued Muller, "you said yourself that when the gentleman's parents died, Mrs. Bernauer was a fine active woman, therefore I supposed she was no longer so."

Franz thought the matter over for a while. "I don't know just why I put it that way. Indeed she's still as active as ever and always fresh and well. It's true that for the last two or three days she's been very nervous and since yesterday it is as if she was a changed woman. She must be ill, I don't know how to explain it otherwise."

"What seems to be the matter with her?" asked Muller and then to explain his interest in the housekeeper's health, he fabricated a story: "I studied medicine at one time and although I didn't finish my course or get a diploma, I've always had a great interest in such things, and every now and then I'll take a case, particularly nervous diseases. That was my specialty." Muller took up his glass and turned away from the window, for he felt a slow flush rising to his cheeks. It was another of Muller's peculiarities that he always felt an inward embarrassment at the lies he was obliged to tell in his profession.

The butler did not seem to have noticed it however, and appeared eager to tell of what concerned him in the housekeeper's appearance and demeanour. "Why, yesterday at dinner time was the first that we began to notice anything wrong with Mrs. Bernauer. The rest of us, that is, Lizzie the upstairs girl, the cook and myself. She began to eat her dinner with a good appetite, then suddenly, when we got as far as the pudding, she let her fork fall and turned deathly white. She got up without saying a word and left the room. Lizzie ran after her to ask if anything was the matter, but she said no, it was nothing of importance. After dinner, she went right out, saying she was doing some errands. She brought in a lot of newspapers, which was quite unusual, for she sometimes does not look at a newspaper once a week even. I wouldn't have noticed it but Lizzie's the kind that sees and hears everything and she told us about it." Franz stopped to take a drink, and Muller said indifferently, "I suppose Mrs. Bernauer was interested in the murder case. The whole neighbourhood seems to be aroused about it."

"No, I don't think that was it," answered the old servant, "because then she would have sent for a paper this morning too."

"And she didn't do that?"

"No, unless she might have gone out for it herself. There's a news stand right next door here. But I don't think she did because I would have seen the paper around the house then."

"And is that all that's the matter with her?" asked Muller in a tone of disappointment. "Why, I thought you'd have something really interesting to tell me."

"Oh, no, that isn't all, sir," exclaimed the old man eagerly.

Muller leaned forward, really interested now, while Franz continued: "She was uneasy all the afternoon yesterday. She walked up and down stairs and through the halls — I remember Lizzie making some joke about it — and then in the evening to our surprise she suddenly began a great rummaging in the first story."

"Is that where she lives?"

"Oh, no; her room is in the wing out towards the garden. The rooms on the first floor all belong to the master and mistress. This morning we found out that Mrs. Bernauer's cleaning up of the evening before had been done because she remembered that the master wanted to take some papers with him but couldn't find them and had asked her to look for them and send them right on."

"Well, I shouldn't call that a sign of any particular nervousness, but rather an evidence of Mrs. Bernaner's devotion to her duty."

"Oh, yes, sir — but it certainly is queer that she should go into the garden at four o'clock this morning and appear to be looking for something along the paths and under the bushes. Even if a few of the papers blew out of the window, or blew away from the summer house, where the master writes sometimes, they couldn't have scattered all over the garden like that."

Muller didn't follow up this subject any longer. There might come a time when he would be interested in finding out the reason for the housekeeper's search in the garden, but just at present he wanted something else. He remembered some remark of the old man's about the "poor little dog," and on this he built his plan.

"Oh, well," he said carelessly, "almost everybody is nervous and impatient now-a-days. I suppose Mrs. Bernauer felt uneasy because she couldn't find the paper right away. There's nothing particularly interesting or noticeable about that. Anyway, I've been occupying myself much more these last years with sick animals rather than with sick people. I've had some very successful cures there."

"No, really, have you? Then you could do us a great favour," exclaimed Franz in apparent eagerness. Muller's heart rejoiced. He had apparently hit it right this time. He knew that in a house like that "a poor dog" could only mean a "sick dog." But his voice was quite calm as he asked: "How can I do you a favour?"

"Why, you see, sir, we've got a little terrier," explained the old man, who had quite forgotten the fact that he had mentioned the dog before. "And there's been something the matter with the poor little chap for several days. He won't eat or drink, he bites at the grass and rolls around on his stomach and cries — it's a pity to see him. If you're fond of animals and know how to take care of them, you may be able to help us there."

"You want me to look at the little dog? Why, yes, I suppose I can."

"We'll appreciate it," said the old man with an embarrassed smile. But Muller shook his head and continued: "No, never mind the payment, I wouldn't take any money for it. But I'll tell you what you can do for me. I'm very fond of flowers. If you think you can take the responsibility of letting me walk around in the garden for a little while, and pick a rose or two, I will be greatly pleased."

"Why, of course you may," said Franz. "Take any of the roses you see there that please you. They're nearly over for the season now and it's better they should be picked rather than left to fade on the bush. We don't use so many flowers in the house now when the family are not there."

"All right, then, it's a bargain," laughed Muller, signalling to the landlord. "Are you, going already?" asked the old servant.

"Yes, I must be going if I am to spend any time with the little dog."

"I suppose I ought to be at home myself," said Franz. "Something's the matter with the electric wiring in our place. The bell in the master's room keeps ringing. I wrote to Siemens & Halske to send us a man out to fix it. He's likely to come any minute now." The two men rose, paid their checks, and went out together. Outside the cafe Muller hesitated a moment. "You go on ahead," he said to Franz. "I want to go in here and get a cigar."

While buying his cigar and lighting it, he asked for several newspapers, choosing those which his quick eye had told him were no longer among the piles on the counter. "I'm very sorry, sir," said the clerk; "we have only a few of those papers, just two or three more than we need for our regular customers, and this morning they are all sold. The housekeeper from the Thorne mansion took the very last ones."

This was exactly what Muller wanted to know. He left the store and caught up with the old butler as the latter was opening the handsome iron gate that led from the Thorne property out onto the street.

"Well, where's our little patient?" asked the

detective as he walked through the courtyard with Franz.

"You'll see him in a minute," answered the old servant. He led the way through a light roomy corridor furnished with handsome old pieces in empire style, and opened a door at its further end.

"This is my room."

It was a large light room with two windows opening on the garden. Muller was not at all pleased that the journey through the hall had been such a short one. However he was in the house, that was something, and he could afford to trust to chance for the rest. Meanwhile he would look at the dog. The little terrier lay in a corner by the stove and it did not take Muller more than two or three minutes to discover that there was nothing the matter with the small patient but a simple case of over-eating. But he put on a very wise expression as he handled the little dog and looking up, asked if he could get some chamomile tea.

"I'll go for it, I think there's some in the house. Do you want it made fresh?" said Franz.

"Yes, that will be better, about a cupful will do," was Muller's answer. He knew that this harmless remedy would be likely to do the dog good and at the present moment he wanted to be left alone in the room. As soon as Franz had gone, the detective hastened to the window, placing himself behind the curtain so that he could not be seen from outside. He himself could see first a wide courtyard lying between the two wings of the house, then beyond it the garden, an immense square plot of ground beautifully cultivated. The left wing of the house was about six windows longer than the other, and from the first story of it it would be quite easy to look out over the vacant lot where the old shed stood which had served as a night's lodging for Johann Knoll.

There was not the slightest doubt in Muller's mind that this part of the tramp's story was true, for by a natural process of elimination he knew there was nothing to be gained by inventing any such tale. Besides which the detective himself had been to look at the shed. His well-known pedantic thoroughness would not permit him to take any one's word for anything that he might find out for himself, In his investigations on Tuesday morning he had already seen the half-ruined shed, now he knew that it contained a broken bench.

Thus far, therefore, Knoll's story was proved to be true-but there was something that didn't quite hitch in another way. The tramp had said that he had seen first a woman and then a man come from the main house and go in the direction of the smaller house which he took to be the gardener's dwelling. This Muller discovered now was quite impossible. A tall hedge, fully seven or eight feet high and very thick, stretched from the courtyard far down into the garden past the gardener's little house. There was a broad path on the right and the left of this green wall. From his position in the shed, Knoll could have seen people passing only when they were on the right side of the hedge. But to reach the gardener's house from the main dwelling, the shortest way would be on the left side of the hedge. This much Muller saw, then he heard the butler's steps along the hall and he went back to the corner where the dog lay.

Franz was not alone. There was some one else with him, the housekeeper, Mrs. Bernauer. Just as they opened the door, Muller heard her say: "If the gentleman is a veterinary, then we'd better ask him about the parrot — "

The sentence was never finished. Muller never found out what was the matter with the parrot, for as he looked up with a polite smile of interest, he looked into a pale face, into a pair of eyes that opened wide in terror, and heard trembling lips frame the words: "There he is again!"

A moment later Mrs. Bernauer would have been glad to have recalled her exclamation, but it was too late.

Muller bowed before her and asked: "'There he is again,' you said; have you ever seen me before?"

The woman looked at him as if hypnotised and answered almost in a whisper: "I saw you

Tuesday morning for the first time, Tuesday morning when the family were going away. Then I saw you pass through our street twice again that same day. This morning you went past the garden gate and now I find you here. What-what is it you want of us?"

"I will tell you what I want, Mrs. Bernauer, but first I want to speak to you alone. Mr. Franz doesn't mind leaving us for a while, does he?"

"But why?" said the old man hesitatingly. He didn't understand at all what was going on and he would much rather have remained.

"Because I came here for the special purpose of speaking to Mrs. Bernauer," replied Muller calmly.

"Then you didn't come on account of the dog?"

"No, I didn't come on account of the dog."

"Then you — you lied to me?"

"Partly."

"And you're no veterinary?"

"No — I can help your dog, but I am not a veterinary and never have been."

"What are you then?"

"I will tell Mrs. Bernauer who and what I am when you are outside — outside in the courtyard there. You can walk about in the garden if you want to, or else go and get some simple purgative for this dog. That is all he needs; he has been over-fed."

Franz was quite bewildered. These new developments promised to be interesting and he was torn between his desire to know more, and his doubts as to the propriety of leaving the housekeeper with this queer stranger. He hesitated until the woman herself motioned to him to go. He went out into the hall, then into the courtyard, watched by the two in the room who stood silently in the window until they saw the butler pass down into the garden. Then they looked at each other.

"You belong to the police?" asked Adele Bernauer finally with a deep sigh.

"That was a good guess," replied Muller with an ironic smile, adding: "All who have any reason to fear us are very quick in recognising us."

"What do you mean by that?" she exclaimed with a start. "What are you thinking of?"

"I am thinking about the same thing that you are thinking of — that I have proved you are thinking of — the same thing that drove you out into the street yesterday and this morning to buy the papers. These papers print news which is interesting many people just now, and some people a great deals. I am thinking of the same thing that was evidently in your thoughts as you peered out of the garden gate this morning, although you would not come out into the street. I know that you do not read even one newspaper regularly. I know also that yesterday and today you bought a great many papers, apparently to get every possible detail about a certain subject. Do you deny this?"

She did not deny it, she did not answer at all. She sank down on a chair, her wide staring eyes looking straight ahead of her, and trembling so that the old chair cracked underneath her weight. But this condition did not last long. The woman had herself well under control. Muller's coming, or something else, perhaps, may have overwhelmed her for a moment, but she soon regained her usual self-possession.

"Still you have not told me what you want here," she began coldly, and as he did not answer she continued: "I have a feeling that you are watching us. I had this feeling when I saw you the first time and noticed then — pardon my frankness — that you stared at us sharply while we were saying goodbye to our master and mistress. Then I saw you pass twice again through the street and look up at our windows. This morning I find you at our garden gate and now — you will pardon me if I tell the exact truth — now you have wormed yourself in here under false pretenses because you have no right whatever to force an entrance into this house. And I ask you again, what do you want here?"

Muller was embarrassed. That did not happen very often. Also it did not happen very often that he was in the wrong as he was now. The woman was absolutely right. He had wormed himself into the house under false pretenses to follow up the new clue which almost unconsciously as yet was leading him on with a stronger and stronger attraction. He could not have explained it and he certainly was not ready to say anything about it at police headquarters, even at the risk of being obliged to continue to enter this mysterious house under false pretenses and to be told that he was doing so. Of course this sort of thing was necessary in his business, it was the only way in which he could follow up the criminals.

But there was something in this woman's words that cut into a sensitive spot and drove the blood to his cheeks. There was something in the bearing and manner of this one-time nurse that impressed him, although he was not a man to be lightly impressed. He had a feeling that he had made a fool of himself and it bothered him. For a moment he did not know what he should say to this woman who stood before him with so much quiet energy in her bearing. But the something in his brain, the something that made him what he was, whispered to him that he had done right, and that he must follow up the trail he had found. That gave him back his usual calm.

He took up his hat, and standing before the pale-faced woman, looking her firmly in the eyes, he said: "It is true that I have no right as yet to force my way into your house, therefore I have been obliged to enter it as best I could. I have done this often in my work, but I do it for the safety of society. And those who reproach me for doing it are generally those whom I have been obliged to persecute in the name of the law. Mrs. Bernauer, I will confess that there are moments in which I feel ashamed that I have chosen this profession that compels me to hunt down human beings. But I do not believe that this is one of those moments. You have read this morning's papers; you must know, therefore, that a man has been arrested and accused of the murder which interests you so much; you must be able to realise the terror and anxiety which are now filling this man's heart. For to-day's papers — I have read them myself — expressed the public sentiment that the police may succeed in convicting this man of the crime, that the death may be avenged and justice have her due. Several of these papers, the papers I know you have bought and presumably read, do not doubt that Johann Knoll is the murderer of Leopold Winkler.

"Now there are at least two people who do not believe that Knoll is the murderer. I am one of them, and you, Mrs. Bernauer, you are the other. I am going now and when I come again, as I doubtless will come again, I will come with full right to enter this house. I acknowledge frankly that I have no justification in causing your arrest as yet, but you are quite clever enough to know that if I had the faintest justification I would not leave here alone. And one thing more I have to say. You may not know that I have had the most extraordinary luck in my profession, that in more than a hundred cases there have been but two where the criminal I was hunting escaped me. And now, Mrs. Bernauer, I will bid you good day."

Muller stepped towards the window and motioned to Franz, who was walking up and down outside. The old man ran to the door and met the detective in the hall.

"You'd better go in and look after Mrs. Bernauer," said the latter, "I can find my way out alone."

Franz looked after him, shaking his head in bewilderment and then entered his own room. "Merciful God!" he exclaimed, bending down in terror over the housekeeper, who lay on the floor. In his shock and bewilderment he imagined that she too had been murdered, until he realised that it was only a swoon from which she recovered in a moment. He helped her regain her feet and she looked about as if still dazed, stammering: "Has he gone?"

"The strange man? ... Yes, he went some time ago. But what happened to you? Did he give you something to make you faint? Do you think he was a thief?"

Mrs. Bernauer shook her head and murmured: "Oh, no, quite the contrary." A remark which did not enlighten Franz particularly as to the status of the man who had just left them. There was a note of fear in the housekeepers's voice and she added hastily: "Does any one besides ourselves know that he was here?"

"No, Lizzie and the cook are in the kitchen talking about the murder."

Mrs. Bernauer shivered again and went slowly out of the room and up the stairs.

If Franz believed that the stranger had left the house by the front entrance he was very much mistaken. When Muller found himself alone in the corridor he turned quickly and hurried out into the garden. None of the servants had seen him. Lizzie and the cook were engaged in an earnest conversation in the kitchen and Franz was fully occupied with Mrs. Bernauer. The gardener was away and his wife busy at her wash tubs. No one was aware, therefore, that Muller spent about ten minutes wandering about the garden, and ten minutes were quite sufficient for him to become so well acquainted with the place that he could have drawn a map of it. He left the garden through the rear gate, the latch of which he was obliged to leave open. The gardener's wife found it that way several hours later and was rather surprised thereat. Muller walked down the street rapidly and caught a passing tramway. His mood was not of the best, for he could not make up his mind whether or no this morning had been a lost one. His mind sorted and rearranged all that he knew or could imagine concerning Mrs. Bernaner. But there was hardly enough of these facts to reassure him that he was not on a false trail, that he had not allowed himself to waste precious hours all because he had seen a woman's haggard face appear for a moment at the little gate in the quiet street.

CHAPTER VIII. JOHANN KNOLL REMEMBERS SOMETHING ELSE

Muller's goal was the prison where Johann Knoll was awaiting his fate. The detective had permission to see the man as often as he wished to. Knoll had been proven a thief, but the accusation of murder against him had not been strengthened by anything but the most superficial circumstantial evidence, therefore it was necessary that Muller should talk with him in the hope of discovering something more definite.

Knoll lay asleep on his cot as the detective and the warder entered the cell. Muller motioned the attendant to leave him alone with the prisoner and he stood beside the cot looking down at the man. The face on the hard pillow was not a very pleasant one to look at. The skin was roughened and swollen and had that brown-purple tinge which comes from being constantly in the open air, and from habitual drinking. The weather-beaten look may be seen often in the faces of men whose honest work keeps them out of doors; but this man had not earned his colouring honestly, for he was one of the sort who worked only from time to time when it was absolutely necessary and there was no other way of getting a penny. His hands proved this, for although soiled and grimy they had soft, slender fingers which showed no signs of a life of toil. But even a man who has spent forty years in useless idling need not be all bad. There must have been some good left in this man or he could not have lain there so quietly, breathing easily, wrapped in a slumber as undisturbed as that of a child. It did not seem possible that any man could lie there like that with the guilt of murder on his conscience, or even with the knowledge in his soul that he had plundered a corpse.

Muller had never believed the first to be the case, but he had thought it possible that Knoll knew perfectly well that it was a lifeless body he was robbing. He had believed it at least until the moment when he stood looking down at the sleeping tramp. Now, with the deep knowledge of the human heart which was his by instinct and which his profession had increased a thousand-fold, Muller knew that this man before him had no heavy crime upon his conscience — that it was really as he had said — that he had taken the watch and purse from one whom he believed to be intoxicated only. Of course it was not a very commendable deed for which the tramp was now in prison, but it was slight in comparison to the crimes of which he was suspected.

Muller bent lower over the unconscious form and was surprised to see a gentle smile spread over the face before him. It brightened and changed the coarse rough face and gave it for a moment a look of almost child-like innocence. Somewhere within the coarsened soul there must be a spot of brightness from which such a smile could come.

But the face grew ugly again as Knoll opened his eyes and looked up. He shook off the clouds of slumber as he felt Muller's hand on his shoulder and raised himself to a sitting position, grumbling: "Can't I have any rest? Are they going to question me again? I'm getting tired of this. I've said everything I know anyhow."

"Perhaps not everything. Perhaps you will answer a few of my questions when I tell you that I believe the story you told us yesterday, and that I want to be your friend and help you."

Knoll's little eyes glanced up without embarrassment at the man who spoke to him. They were sharp eyes and had a certain spark of intelligence in them. Muller had noticed that yesterday, and he saw it again now. But he saw also the gleam of distrust in these eyes, a distrust which found expression in Knoll's next words. "You think you can catch me with your good words, but you're makin' a mistake. I've got nothin' new to say. And you needn't think that you can blind me, I know you're one of the police, and I'm not going to say anything at all."

"Just as you like. I was trying to help you, I believe I really could help you. I have just come from Hietzing — but of course if you don't want to talk to me — " Muller shrugged his shoulders and turned toward the door.

But before he reached it Knoll stood at his side. "You really mean to help me?" he gasped.

"I do," said the detective calmly.

"Then swear, on your mother's soul — or is your mother still alive?"

"No, she has been dead some time."

"Well, then, will you swear it?"

"Would you believe an oath like that?"

"Why shouldn't I?"

"With the life you've been leading?"

"My life's no worse than a lot of others. Stealing those things on Monday was the worst thing I've done yet. Will you swear?"

"Is it something so very important you have to tell me?"

"No, I ain't got nothin' at all new to tell you. But I'd just like to know — in this black hole I've got into — I'd just like to know that there's one human being who means well with me — I'd like to know that there's one man in the world who don't think I'm quite good-for-nothin'."

The tramp covered his face with his hands and gave a heart-rending sob. Deep pity moved the detective's breast. He led Knoll back to his cot, and put both hands on his shoulders, saying gravely: "I believe that this theft was the worst thing you have done. By my mother's salvation, Knoll, I believe your words and I will try to help you."

Knoll raised his head, looking up at Muller with a glance of unspeakable gratitude. With trembling lips he kissed the hand which a moment before had pressed kindly on his shoulder, clinging fast to it as if he could not bear to let it go. Muller was almost embarrassed. "Oh, come now, Knoll, don't be foolish. Pull yourself together and answer my questions carefully, for I am asking you these questions more for your own sake than for anything else."

The tramp nodded and wiped the tears from his face. He looked almost happy again, and there was a softness in his eyes that showed there was something in the man which might be saved and which was worth saving.

Muller sat beside him on the cot and began: "There was one mistake in your story yesterday. I want you to think it over carefully. You said that you saw first a woman and then a man going through the neighbouring garden. I believe that one or both of these people is the criminal for whom we are looking. Therefore, I want you to try and remember everything that you can connect with them, every slightest detail. Anything that you can tell us may be of the greatest importance. Therefore, think very carefully."

Knoll sat still a few moments, evidently trying hard to put his hazy recollections into useful form and shape. But it was also evident that orderly thinking was an unusual work for him, and he found it almost too difficult. "I guess you 'better ask me questions, maybe that'll go," he said after a pause.

Then Muller began to question. With his usual thoroughness he began at the very beginning: "When was it that you climbed the fence to get into the shed?"

"It just struck nine o'clock when I put my foot on the lowest bar."

"Are you sure of that?"

"Quite sure. I counted every stroke. You see, I wanted to know how long the night was going to be, seein' I'd have to sleep in that shed. I was in the garden just exactly an hour. I came out of the shed as it struck ten and it wasn't but a few minutes before I was in the street again."

"And when was it that you saw the woman in the garden next door?"

"H'm, I don't just know when that was. I'd been in on the bench quite a while."

"And the man? When did you see the man?"

"He came past a few minutes after the woman had gone towards the little house in the garden."

"Ah! there you see, that's where you made your mistake. It is more than likely that these two did not go to the little house, but that they went somewhere else. Did they walk slowly and quietly?"

"Not a bit of it. They ran almost... Went past as quick as a bat in the night."

"Then they both appeared to be in a hurry?"

"Yes indeed they did."

"Ah, ha, you see! Now when any one's in a hurry he doesn't go the longest way round, as a rule. And it would have been the longest way round for these two people to go from the big house to the gardener's cottage — for the little house you saw was the gardener's cottage. There is tall thick hedge that starts from the main building and goes right down through the garden, quite a distance past the gardener's cottage. The vegetable garden is on the left side of this hedge and in the middle of the vegetable garden is the gardener's cottage. But you could have seen the man and the woman only because they passed down the right side of the hedge, and this would have given them a detour of fifty paces or more to reach the gardener's house. Nov do you think that two people who were very much in a hurry would have gone down the right side of the hedge, to reach a place which they could have gotten to much quicker on the left side?"

"No, that would have been a fool thing to do."

"And you are quite sure that these people were in a hurry?"

"That's dead sure. I scarcely saw them before

they'd gone again."

"And you didn't see them come back?"

"No, at least I didn't pay any further attention to them. When I thought it wouldn't be any
good to look about in there I turned around and
dozed off."

"And it was during this dozing that you
thought you heard the shot?"

"Yes, sir, that's right."

"And you didn't notice anything else? You
didn't hear anything else."

"No, nothin' at all, there was so much noise
anyway. There was a high wind that night and
the trees were rattling and creaking."

"And you didn't see anything else, anything
that attracted your attention?"

"No, nothing — " Knoll did not finish his sentence, but began another instead. He had suddenly remembered something which had seemed
to him of no importance before. "There was a
light that went out suddenly."

"Where?"

"In the side of the house that I could see from
my place. There was a lamp in the last window of
the second story, a lamp with a red shade. That
lamp went out all at once."

"Was the window open?"

"Yes."

"There was a strong wind that night, might not the wind have blown the lamp out?"

"No, that wasn't it," said Knoll, rising hastily.

"Well, how was it?" asked Muller calmly.

"A hand put out the lamp."

"Whose hand?"

"I couldn't see that. The light was so low on account of the shade that I couldn't see the person who stood there."

"And you don't know whether it was a man or a woman?"

"No, I just saw a hand, more like a shadow it was."

"Well, it doesn't matter much anyway. It was after nine o'clock and many people go to bed about that time," said Muller, who did not see much value in this incident.

But Knoll shook his head. "The person who put out that light didn't go to bed, at least not right away," he said eagerly. "I looked over after a while to the place where the red light was and I saw something else."

"Well, what was it you saw?"

"The window had been closed."

"Who closed it? Didn't you see the person

that time? The moonlight lay full on the house."

"Yes, when there weren't any clouds. But there was a heavy cloud over the moon just then and when it came out again the window was shut and there was a white curtain drawn in front of it."

"How could you see that?"

"I could see it when the lamp was lit again."

"Then the lamp was lit again?"

"Yes, I could see the red light behind the curtain."

"And what happened then?"

"Nothing more then, except that the man went through the garden."

Muller rose now and took up his hat. He was evidently excited and Knoll looked at him uneasily. "You're goin' already?" he asked.

"Yes, I have a great deal to do to-day," replied the detective and nodded to the prisoner as he knocked on the door. "I am glad you remembered that," he added, "it will be of use to us, I think."

The warder opened the door, let Muller out, and the heavy iron portal clanged again between Knoll and freedom.

Muller was quite satisfied with the result of his visit to the accused. He hurried to the nearest

cab stand and entered one of the carriages waiting there. He gave the driver Mrs. Klingmayer's
address. It was about two o'clock in the afternoon
now and Muller had had nothing to eat yet. But
he was quite unaware of the fact as his mind was
so busy that no mere physical sensation could
divert his attention for a moment. Muller never
seemed to need sleep or food when he was on the
trail, particularly not in the fascinating first stages
of the case when it was his imagination alone,
catching at trifles unnoticed by others, combining
them in masterly fashion to an ordered whole,
that first led the seekers to the truth. Now he
went over once more all the little apparently trivial incidents that had caused him first to watch
the Thorne household and then had drawn his
attention, and his suspicion, to Adele Bernauer. It
was the broken willow twig that had first drawn
his attention to the old garden next the Thorne
property. This twig, this garden, and perhaps
some one who could reach his home again, unseen and unendangered through this garden —
might not this have something to do with the
murder?

The breaking of the twig was already explained. It was Johann Knoll who had stepped on
it. But he had not climbed the wall at all, had only
crept along it looking for a night's shelter. And
there was no connection between Knoll and the
people who lived in the Thorne house. Muller
had not the slightest doubt that the tramp had
told the entire truth that day and the day preced-

ing.

Then the detective's mind went back to the happenings of Tuesday morning. The little twig had first drawn his attention to the Thorne estate and the people who lived there. He had seen the departure of the young couple and had passed the house again that afternoon and the following day, drawn to it as if by a magnet. He had not been able then to explain what it was that attracted him; there had been nothing definite in his mind as he strolled past the old mansion. But his repeated appearance had been noticed by some one — by one person only — the housekeeper. Why should she have noticed it? Had she any reason for believing that she might be watched? People with an uneasy conscience are very apt to connect even perfectly natural trivial circumstances with their own doings. Adele Bernauer had evidently connected Muller's repeated passing with something that concerned herself even before the detective had thought of her at all.

Muller had not noticed her until he had seen her peculiar conduct that very morning. When he heard Franz's words and saw how disturbed the woman was, he asked himself: "Why did this woman want to be shown the spot of the murder? Didn't she know that place, living so near it, as well as any of the many who stood there staring in morbid curiosity? Did she ask to have it shown her that the others might believe she had nothing whatever to do with the occurrences that had happened there? Or was she drawn thither by that queer attraction that brings the criminal back to the scene of his crime?"

The sudden vision of Mrs. Bernauer's head at the garden gate, and its equally sudden disappearance had attracted Muller's attention and his thoughts to the woman. What he had been able to learn about her had increased his suspicions and her involuntary exclamation when she met him face to face in the house had proved beyond a doubt that there was something on her mind. His open accusation, her demeanour, and finally her swoon, were all links in the chain of evidence that this woman knew something about the murder in the quiet lane.

With this suspicion in his mind what Muller had learned from Knoll was of great value to him, at all events of great interest. Was it the house-keeper who had put out the light? For now Muller did not doubt for a moment that this sudden extinguishing of the lamp was a signal. He believed that Knoll had seen clearly and that he had told truly what he had seen. A lamp that is blown out by the wind flickers uneasily before going out. A sudden extinguishing of the light means human agency. And the lamp was lit again a few moments afterward and burned on steadily as before. A short time after the lamp had been put out the man had been seen going through the garden. And it could not have been much later before the shot was heard. This shot had been fired between the hours of nine and ten, for it was during this hour only that Knoll was in the garden house and heard the shot. But it was not necessary to depend upon the tramp's evidence alone to determine the exact hour of the shot. It must have been before half past nine, or otherwise the janitor of No.1, who came home at that hour and lay awake so long, would undoubtedly have heard a shot fired so near his domicile, in spite of the noise occasioned by the high wind. There would have been sufficient time for Mrs. Bernauer to have reached the place of the murder between the putting out of the lamp and the firing of the shot. But perhaps she may have rested quietly in her room; she may have been only the inciter or the accomplice of the deed. But at all events, she knew something about it, she was in some way connected with it.

Muller drew a deep breath. He felt much easier now that he had arranged his thoughts and marshalled in orderly array all the facts he had already gathered. There was nothing to do now but to follow up a given path step by step and he could no longer reproach himself that he might have cast suspicion on an innocent soul. No, his bearing towards Mrs. Bernauer had not been sheer brutality. His instinct, which had led him so unerringly so many times, had again shown him the right way when he had thrust the accusation in her face.

Now that his mind was easier he realised that he was very hungry. He drove to a restaurant and ordered a hasty meal.

"Beer, sir?' asked the waiter for the third time.

"No," answered Muller, also for the third time.

"Then you'll take wine, sir?" asked the insistent Ganymede.

"Oh, go to the devil! When I want anything I'll ask for it," growled the detective, this time effectively scaring the waiter. It did not often happen that a customer refused drinks, but then there were not many customers who needed as clear, a head as Muller knew he would have to have to-day. Always a light drinker, it was one of his rules never to touch a drop of liquor during this first stage of the mental working out of any new problem which presented itself. But soft-hearted as he was, he repented of his irritation a moment later and soothed the waiter's wounded feelings by a rich tip. The boy ran out to open the cab door for his strange customer and looked after him, wondering whether the man was a cranky millionaire or merely a poet. For Joseph Muller, by name and by reputation one of the best known men in Vienna, was by sight unknown to all except the few with whom he had to do on the police force. His appearance, in every way inconspicuous, and the fact that he never sought acquaintance with any one, was indeed of the greatest possible assistance to him in his work. Many of those who saw him several times in a day would pass him or look him full in the face without recognising him. It was only, as in the case of Mrs. Bernauer, the guilty conscience that remembered face and figure of this quiet-looking man who was one of the most-feared servants of the law in Austria.

CHAPTER IX. THE ELECTRICIAN

When Muller reached the house where Mrs. Klingmayer lived he ordered the cabman to wait and hurried up to the widow's little apartment. He had the key to Leopold Winkler's room in his own pocket, for Mrs. Klingmayer had given this key to Commissioner von Riedau at the latter's request and the commissioner had given it to Muller. The detective told the good woman not to bother about him as he wanted to make an examination of the place alone. Left to himself in the little room, Muller made a thorough search of it, opening the cupboard, the bureau drawers, every possible receptacle where any article could be kept or hidden. What he wanted to find was some letter, some bit of paper, some memoranda perhaps, anything that would show any connection existing between the murdered man and Mrs. Bernauer, who lived so near the place where this man had died and who was so greatly interested in his murder.

The detective's search was not quite in vain, although he could not tell yet whether what he had found would be of any value. Leopold Winkler had had very little correspondence, or else he had had no reason to keep the letters he received. Muller found only about a half dozen letters in all. Three of them were from women of the half-world, giving dates for meetings. Another was written by a man and signed "Theo." This "Theo" appeared to be the same sort of a cheap rounder that Winkler was. And he seemed to have sunk one grade deeper than the dead man, in spite of the latter's bad reputation. For this other addressed Winkler as his "Dear Friend" and pleaded with him for "greater discretion," alluding evidently to something which made this discretion necessary.

"I wonder what rascality it was that made these two friends?" murmured Muller, putting Theo's letter with the three he had already read. But before he slipped it in his pocket he glanced at the postmark. The letters of the three women had all been posted from different quarters of the city some months ago. Theo's letter was postmarked "Marburg," and dated on the 1st of September of the present year.

Then Muller looked at the postmark of the two remaining letters which he had not yet read, and whistled softly to himself. Both these letters were posted from a certain station in Hietzing, the station which was nearest his own lodgings and also nearest the Thorne house. He looked at the postmark more sharply. They both bore the dates of the present year, one of them being stamped "March 17th," the other "September 24th." This last letter interested the detective most.

Muller was not of a nervous disposition, but his hand trembled slightly as he took the letter from its envelope. It was clear that this letter had been torn open hastily, for the edges of the opening were jagged and uneven.

When the detective had read the letter — it contained but a few lines and bore neither address nor signature — he glanced over it once more as if to memorise the words. They were as follows: "Do not come again. In a day or two I will be able to do what I have to do. I will send you later news to your office. Impatience will not help you." — These words were written hastily on a piece of paper that looked as if it had been torn from a pad. In spite of the haste the writer had been at some pains to disguise the handwriting. But it was a clumsy disguise, done by one not accustomed to such tricks, and it was evidently done by a woman. All she had known how to do to disguise her writing had been to twist and turn the paper while writing, so that every letter had a different position. The letters were also made unusually long. This peculiarity of the writing was seen on both letters and both envelopes. The earlier letter was still shorter and seemed to have been written with the same haste, and with the same disgust, or perhaps even hatred, for the man to whom it was written.

"Come to-morrow, but not before eight o'clock. He has gone away. God forgive him and you." This was the contents of the letter of the 17th of March. That is, the writer had penned the letter this way. But the last two words, "and you," had evidently not come from her heart, for she had annulled them by a heavy stroke of the pen.

A stroke that seemed like a knife thrust, so full of rage and hate it was.

"So he was called to a rendezvous in Hietzing, too," murmured Muller, then he added after a few moments: "But this rendezvous had nothing whatever to do with love."

There was nothing else in Winkler's room which could be of any value to Muller in the problem that was now before him. And yet he was very well satisfied with the result of his errand.

He entered his cab again, ordering the driver to take him to Hietzing. Just before he had reached the corner where he had told the man to stop, another cab passed them, a coupe, in which was a solitary woman. Muller had just time enough to recognise this woman as Adele Bernauer, and to see that she looked even more haggard and miserable than she had that morning. She did not look up as the other cab passed her carriage, therefore she did not see Muller. The detective looked at his watch and saw that it was almost half-past four. The unexpected meeting changed, his plans for the afternoon. He had decided that he must enter the Thorne mansion again that very day, for he must find out the meaning of the red-shaded lamp. And now that the housekeeper was away it would be easier for him to get into the house, therefore it must be done at once. His excuse was all ready, for he had been weighing possibilities. He dismissed his cab a block from his own home and entered his house cautiously.

Muller's lodgings consisted of two large rooms, really much too large for a lone man who was at home so little. But Muller had engaged them at first sight, for the apartment possessed one qualification which was absolutely necessary for him. Its situation and the arrangement of its doors made it possible for him to enter and leave his rooms without being seen either by his own landlady or by the other lodgers in the house. The little apartment was on the ground floor, and Muller's own rooms had a separate entrance opening on to the main corridor almost immediately behind the door. Nine times out of ten, he could come and go without being seen by any one in the house. To-day was the first time, however, that Muller had had occasion to try this particular qualification of his new lodgings.

He opened the street door and slipped into his own room without having seen or been seen by any one.

Fifteen minutes later he left the apartment again, but left it such a changed man that nobody who had seen him go in would have recognised him. Before he came out, however, he looked about carefully to see whether there was any one in sight He came out unseen and was just closing the main door behind him, when he met the janitress.

"Were you looking for anybody in the house?" said the woman, glancing sharply at the stranger, who answered in a slightly veiled voice: "No, I made a mistake in the number. The place I am looking for is two houses further down."

He walked down the street and the woman looked after him until she saw him turn into the doorway of the second house. Then she went into her own rooms. The house Muller entered happened to be a corner house with an entrance on the other street, through which the detective passed and went on his way. He was quite satisfied with the security of his disguise, for the woman who knew him well had not recognised him at all. If his own janitress did not know him, the people in the Thorne house would never imagine it was he.

And indeed Muller was entirely changed. In actuality small and thin, with sparse brown hair and smooth shaven face, he was now an inch or two taller and very much stouter. He wore thick curly blond hair, a little pointed blond beard and moustache. His eyes were hidden by heavy-rimmed spectacles.

It was just half-past five when he rang the bell at the entrance gate to the Thorne property. He had spent the intervening time in the cafe, as he was in no hurry to enter the house. Franz came down the path and opened the door. "'What do you want?" he asked.

"I come from Siemens & Halske; I was to ask whether the other man — "

"Has been here already?" interrupted Franz, adding in an irritated tone, "No, he hasn't been here at all."

"Well, I guess he didn't get through at the other place in time. I'll see what the trouble is," said the stranger, whom Franz naturally supposed to be the electrician, lie opened the gate and asked the other to come in, leading him into the house. Under a cloudy sky the day was fading rapidly. Muller knew that it would not occur to the real electrician to begin any work as late as this, and that he was perfectly safe in the examination he wanted to make.

"Well, what's the trouble here? Why did you write to our firm?" asked the supposed electrician.

"The wires must cross somewhere, or there's something wrong with the bells. When the housekeeper touches the button in her room to ring for the cook or the upstairs girl, the bell rings in Mr. Thorne's room. It starts ringing and it keeps up with a deuce of a noise. Fortunately the family are away."

"Well, we'll fix it all right for you. First of all I want to look at the button in the housekeeper's room."

"I'll take you up there," said Franz.

They walked through the wide corridor, then turned into a shorter, darker hall and went up a narrow winding stairway. Franz halted before a door in the second story. It was the last of the three doors in the hall. Muller took off his hat as the door opened and murmured a "good-evening."

"There's no one there; Mrs. Bernaner's out."

"Has she gone away, too?" asked the electrician hastily.

Franz did not notice that there was a slight change in the stranger's voice at this question, and he answered calmly as ever: "Oh, no; she's just driven to town. I think she went to see the doctor who lives quite a distance away. She hasn't been feeling at all well. She took a cab to-day. I told her she ought to, as she wasn't well enough to go by the tram. She ought to be home any moment now."

"Well, I'll hurry up with the job so that I'll be out of the way when the lady comes," said Muller, as Franz led him to the misbehaving bell.

It was in the wall immediately above a large table which filled the window niche so completely that there was but scant space left for the comfortable armchair that stood in front of it. The window was open and Muller leaned out, looking down at the garden below.

"What a fine old garden!" he exclaimed

aloud. To himself he said: "This is the last window in the left wing. It is the window where Johann Knoll saw the red light."

And when he turned back into the room again he found the source of this light right at his hand on the handsome old table at which Mrs. Bernauer evidently spent many of her hours. A row of books stood against the wall, framing the back of the table. Well-worn volumes of the classics among them gave proof that the one-time nurse was a woman of education. A sewing basket and neat piles of house linen, awaiting repairs, covered a large part of the table-top, and beside them stood a gracefully shaped lamp, covered by a shade of soft red silk.

It took Muller but a few seconds to see all this. Then he set about his investigation of the electric button. He unscrewed the plate and examined the wires meeting under it. While doing so he cast another glance at the table and saw a letter lying there, an open letter half out of its envelope. This envelope was of unusual shape, long and narrow, and the paper was heavy and high-glossed.

"Your housekeeper evidently has no secrets from the rest of you," Muller remarked with a laugh, still busy at the wires, "or she wouldn't leave her letters lying about like that."

"Oh, we've all heard what's in that letter," replied Franz. "She read it to us when it came this morning. It's from the Madam. She sent messages to all of us and orders, so Mrs. Bernauer read us the whole letter. There's no secrets in that."

"The button has been pressed in too far and caught down. That seems to be the main trouble," said Muller, readjusting the little knob. "I'd like a candle here if I may have one."

"I'll get you a light at once," said Franz. But his intentions, however excellent, seemed difficult of fulfilment. It was rapidly growing dark, and the old butler peered about uncertainly. "Stupid," he muttered. "I don't know where she keeps the matches. I can't find them anywhere. I'm not a smoker, so I haven't any in my pocket."

"Nor I," said Muller calmly, letting his hand close protectingly over a new full box of them in his own pocket.

"I'll get you some from my own room," and Franz hurried away, his loose slippers clattering down the stairs. He was no sooner well out of the room than Muller had the letter in his hand and was standing close by the window to catch the fading light. But on the old servant's return the supposed electrician stood calmly awaiting the coming of the light, and the letter was back on the table half hidden by a piece of linen. Franz did not notice that the envelope was missing. And the housekeeper, whose mind was so upset by the events of the day, and whose thoughts were on other more absorbing matters, would hardly be likely to remember whether she had returned this quite unimportant letter to its envelope or not.

Franz brought a lighted candle with him, and Muller, who really did possess a creditable knowledge of electricity, saw that the wires in the room were all in good condition. As he had seen at first, there was really nothing the matter except with the position of the button. But it did not suit his purpose to enlighten Franz on the matter just yet.

"Now I'd better look at the wires in the gentleman's room," he said, when he had returned plate and button to their place.

"Just as you say," replied Franz, taking up his candle and leading the way out into the hail and down the winding stair. They crossed the lower corridor, mounted another staircase and entered a large, handsomely furnished room, half studio, half library. The wall was covered with pictures and sketches, several easels stood piled up in the corner, and a broad table beside them held paint boxes, colour tubes, brushes, all the paraphernalia of the painter, now carefully ordered and covered for a term of idleness. Great bookcases towered to the ceiling, and a huge flat top desk, a costly piece of furniture, was covered with books and papers. It was the room of a man of brains and breeding, a man of talent and ability, possessing, furthermore, the means to indulge his tastes freely. Even now, with its master absent, the handsome apartment bore the impress of his personality. The detective's quick imagination called up the attractive, sympathetic figure of the man he had seen at the gate, as his quick eye took in the details of the room. All the charm of Herbert Thorne's personality, which the keen-sensed Muller had felt so strongly even in that fleeting glimpse of him, came back again here in the room which was his own little kingdom and the expression of his mentality.

"Well, what's the trouble here? Where are the wires?" asked the detective, after the momentary pause which had followed his entrance into the room. Franz led him to a spot on the wall hidden by a marquetry cabinet. "Here's the bell, it rings for several minutes before it stops."

The light of the candle which the butler held fell upon a portrait hanging above the cabinet. It was a sketch in water-colours, the life-sized head of a man who may have been about thirty years old, perhaps, but who had none of the freshness and vigour of youth. The scanty hair, the sunken temples, and the faded skin, emphasised the look of dissipation given by the lines about the sensual mouth and the shifty eyes.

"Well, say, can't your master find anything better to paint than a face like that?" Muller asked with a laugh.

"Goodness me! you mustn't say such things!" exclaimed Franz in alarm; "that's the Madam's brother. He's an officer, I'd have you know. It's true, he doesn't look like much there, but that's because he's not in uniform. It makes such a difference."

"Is the lady anything like her brother?" asked the detective indifferently, bending to examine the wiring.

"Oh, dear, no, not a bit; they're as different as day and night. He's only her half-brother anyway. She was the daughter of the Colonel's second wife. Our Madam is the sweetest, gentlest lady you can imagine, an angel of goodness. But the Lieutenant here has always been a care to his family, they say. I guess he's quieted down a bit now, for his father — he's Colonel Leining, retired — made him get exchanged from the city to a small garrison town. There's nothing much to do in Marburg, I dare say — well! you are a merry sort, aren't you?" These last words, spoken in a tone of surprise, were called forth by a sudden sharp whistle from the detective, a whistle which went off into a few merry bars.

A sudden whistle like that from Muller's lips was something that made the Imperial Police Force sit up and take notice, for it meant that things were happening, and that the happenings were likely to become exciting. It was a habit he could control only by the severest effort of the will, an effort which he kept for occasions when it was absolutely necessary. Here, alone with the harmless old man, he was not so much on his guard, and the sudden vibrating of every nerve at the word "Marburg," found vent in the whistle which surprised old Franz. One young police commissioner with a fancy for metaphor had likened this sudden involuntary whistle of Muller's to the bay of the hound when he strikes the trail; which was about what it was.

"Yes, I am merry sometimes," he said with a laugh. "It's a habit I have. Something occurred to me just then, something I had forgotten. Hope you don't mind."

"Oh, no, there's no one here now, whistle all you like."

But Muller's whistle was not a continuous performance, and he had now completely mastered the excitation of his nerves which had called it forth. He threw another sharp look at the picture of the man who lived in Marburg, and then asked: "And now where is the button?"

"By the window there, beside the desk." Franz led the way with his candle.

"Why, how funny! What are those mirrors there for?" asked the electrician in a tone of surprise, pointing to two small mirrors hanging in the window niche. They were placed at a height and at such a peculiar angle that no one could possibly see his face in them.

"Something the master is experimenting with, I guess. He's always making queer experiments; he knows a lot about scientific things."

Muller shook his head as if in wonderment, and bent to investigate the button which was fastened into the wall beneath the window sill. His quick ear heard a carriage stopping in front of the house, and heard the closing of the front door a moment later. To facilitate his examination of the button, the detective had seated himself in the armchair which stood beside the desk. He half raised himself now to let the light of the candle fall more clearly on the wiring — then he started up altogether and threw a hasty glance at the mirrors above his head. A ray of light had suddenly flashed down upon him — a ray of red light, and it came reflected from the mirrors. Muller bit his lips to keep back the betraying whistle.

"What's the matter?" asked the butler. "Did you drop anything?"

"Yes, the wooden rim of the button," replied Muller, telling the truth this time. For he had held the little wooden circlet in his hands at the moment when the red light, reflected down from the mirrors, struck full upon his eyes. He had dropped it in his surprise and excitement. Franz found the little ring in the centre of the room where it had rolled, and the supposed electrician replaced it and rose to his feet, saying: "There, I've finished now."

Franz did not recognise the double meaning in the words. "Yes, it's all right! I've finished here now," Muller repeated to himself. For now he knew beyond a doubt that the red light was a signal — and he knew also for whom this signal was intended. It was a signal for Herbert Thorne! — Herbert Thorne, whom no single thought or suspicion of Muller's had yet connected with the murder of Leopold Winkler.

The detective was very much surprised and greatly excited. But Franz did not notice it, and indeed a far keener observer than the slow-witted old butler might have failed to see the sudden gleam which shot up in the grey eyes behind the heavy spectacles, might have failed to notice the tightening of the lips beneath the blond moustache, or the tenseness of the slight frame under the assumed embonpoint. Muller's every nerve was tingling, but he had himself completely in hand.

"What do we owe you?" asked Franz.

"They'll send you a bill from the office. It won't amount to much. I must be getting on now."

Muller hastened out of the door and down the street to the nearest cab stand. There were not very many cab stands in this vicinity, and the detective reasoned that Mrs. Bernauer would naturally have taken her cab from the nearest station. He had heard her return in her carriage, presumably the same in which she had started out.

There was but one cab at the stand. Muller walked to it and laid his hand on the door.

"Oh, Jimmy! must I go out again?" asked the driver hoarsely. "Can't you see the poor beast is all wet from the last ride? We've just come in." He pointed with his whip to the tired-looking animal under his blanket.

"Why, he does look warm. You must have been making a tour out into the country," said the blond gentleman in a friendly tone.

"No, sir, not quite so far as that. I've just taken a woman to the main telegraph office in the city and back again. But she was in a hurry and he's not a young horse, sir."

"Well, never mind, then; I can get another cab across the bridge," replied the stout blond man, turning away and strolling off leisurely in the direction of the bridge. It was now quite dark, and a few steps further on Muller could safely turn and take the road to his own lodging. No one saw him go in, and in a few moments the real Muller, slight, smooth-shaven, sat down at his desk, looking at the papers that lay before him. They were three letters and an empty envelope.

He took up the last, and compared it carefully with the envelope of one of the letters found in Winkler's room — the unsigned letter postmarked Hietzing, September 24th. The two envelopes were exactly alike. They were of the same size and shape, made of the same cream-tinted, heavy, glossy paper, and the address was written by the same hand. This any keen observer, who need not necessarily be an expert, could see. The same hand which had addressed the envelope to Mrs. Adele Bernauer on the letter which was postmarked "Venice," about thirty-six hours previous — this hand had, in an awkward and childish attempt at disguise, written Winkler's address on the envelope which bore the date of September 24th.

The writer of the harmless letter to Mrs. Bernauer, a letter which chatted of household topics and touched lightly on the beauties of Venice, was Mrs. Thorne. It was Mrs. Thorne, therefore, who, reluctantly and in anger and distaste, had called Leopold Winkler to Hietzing, to his death.

And whose hand had fired the shot that caused his death? The question, at this stage in Muller's meditation, could hardly be called a question any more. It was all too sadly clear to him now. Winkler met his death at the hand of the husband, who, discovering the planned rendezvous, had misunderstood its motive.

For truly this had been no lovers' meeting. It had been a meeting to which the woman was driven by fear and hate; the man by greed of gain. This was clearly proved by the 300 guldens found in the dead man's pocket, money enclosed in a delicate little envelope, sealed hastily, and crumpled as if it had been carried in a hot and trembling hand.

It was already known that Winkler never

had any money except at certain irregular intervals, when he appeared to have come into possession of considerable sums. During these days he indulged in extravagant pleasures and spent his money with a recklessness which proved that he had not earned it by honest work.

Leopold Winkler was a blackmailer.

Colonel Leining, retired, the father of two such widely different children, was doubtless a man of stern principles, and an army officer as well, therefore a man with a doubly sensitive code of honour and a social position to maintain; and this man, morbidly sensitive probably, had a daughter who had inherited his sensitiveness and his high ideals of honour, a daughter married to a rich husband. But he had another child, a son without any sense of honour at all, who, although also an officer, failed to live in a manner worthy his position. This son was now in Marburg, where there were no expensive pleasures, no all-night cafes and gambling dens, for a man to lose his time in, his money, and his honour also.

For such must have been the case with Colonel Leining's son before his exile to Marburg. The old butler had hinted at the truth. The portrait drawn by Herbert Thorne, a picture of such technical excellence that it was doubtless a good likeness also, had given an ugly illustration to Franz's remarks. And there was something even more tangible to prove it: "Theo's" letter from Marburg pleading with Winkler for "discretion and silence," not knowing ("let us hope he did not know!" murmured Muller between set teeth) that the man who held him in his power because of some rascality, was being paid for his silence by the Lieutenant's sister.

It is easy to frighten a sensitive woman, so easy to make her believe the worst! And there is little such a tender-hearted woman will not do to save her aging father from pain and sorrow, perhaps even disgrace!

It must have been in this way that Mrs. Thorne came into the power of the scoundrel who paid with his life for his last attempt at blackmail.

When Muller reached this point in his chain of thought, he closed his eyes and covered his face with his hands, letting two pictures stand out clear before his mental vision.

He saw the little anxious group around the carriage in front of the Thorne mansion. He saw the pale, frail woman leaning back on the cushions, and the husband bending over her in tender care. And then he saw Johann Knoll in his cell, a man with little manhood left in him, a man sunk to the level of the brutes, a man who had already committed one crime against society, and who could never rise to the mental or spiritual standard of even the most mediocre of decent citizens.

If Herbert Thorne were to suffer the just punishment for his deed of doubly blind jealousy, then it was not only his own life, a life full of gracious promise, that would be ruined, but the happiness of his delicate, sweet-faced wife, who was doubtless still in blessed ignorance of what had happened. And still one other would be dragged down by this tragedy; a respected, upright man would bow his white hairs in disgrace. Thorne's father-in-law could not escape the scandal and his own share in the responsibility for it. And to a veteran officer, bred in the exaggerated social ethics of his profession, such a disgrace means ruin, sometimes even voluntary death.

"Oh, dear, if it had only been Knoll who did it," said Muller with a sigh that was almost a groan.

Then he rose slowly and heavily, and slowly and heavily, as if borne down by the weight of great weariness, he reached for his hat and coat and left the house.

Whether he wished it or not, he knew it was his duty to go on to the bitter end on this trail he had followed up all day from the moment that he caught that fleeting glimpse of Mrs. Bernauer's haggard face at the garden gate. He was almost angry with the woman, because she chanced to look out of the gate at just that moment, showing him her face distorted with anxiety. For it was her face that had drawn Muller to the trail, a trail at the end of which misery awaited those for whom this woman had worked for years, those whom she loved and who treated her as one of the family.

Muller knew now that the one-time nurse was in league with her former charge; that Thorne and Adele Bernauer were in each other's confidence; that the man sat waiting for the signal which she was to give him, a signal bringing so much disgrace and sorrow in its train.

If the woman had not spied upon and betrayed her mistress, this terrible event, which now weighed upon her own soul, would not have happened.

"A faithful servant, indeed," said Muller, with a harsh laugh.

Then maturer consideration came and forced him to acknowledge that it was indeed devotion that had swayed Adele Bernauer, devotion to her master more than to her mistress. This was hardly to be wondered at. But she had not thought what might come from her revelations, what had come of them. For now her pet, the baby who had once lain in her arms, the handsome, gifted man whom she adored with more than the love of many a mother for the child of her own blood, was under the shadow of hideous disgrace and doom, was the just prey of the law for open trial and condemnation as a murderer.

Muller sighed deeply once more and then came one of those moments which he had spoken of to the unhappy woman that very day. He felt like cursing the fatal gift that was his, the gift to see what was hidden from others, this something within him that forced him relentlessly onward until he had uncovered the truth, and brought misery to many.

Muller need not do anything, he need simply do nothing. Not a soul besides himself suspected the dwellers in the Thorne mansion of any connection with the murder. If he were silent, nothing could be proven against Knoll after all, except the robbery which he himself had confessed. Then the memory of the terror in the tramp's little reddened eyes came back to the detective's mind.

"A human soul after all, and a soul trembling in the shadow of a great fear. And even he's a better man than the blackmailer who was killed. A miscarriage of justice will often make a criminal of a poor fellow whose worst fault is idleness." Muller's face darkened as the things of the past, shut down in the depths of his own soul, rose up again. "No; that's why I took up this work. Justice must be done — but it's bitter hard sometimes. I could almost wish now that I hadn't seen that face at the gate."

CHAPTER X. MULLER RETURNS TO THE THORNE MANSION

It was striking eight as Muller came out of a cafe in the heart of the city. He had been in there but a few moments, for his purpose was merely to look through the Army lists of the current year. The result of his search proved the correctness of his conclusions.

There was a Lieutenant Theobald Leining in the single infantry regiment stationed at Marburg.

Muller took a cab and drove to the main telegraph office. He asked for the original of the telegram which had been sent that afternoon to the address; "Herbert Thorne, Hotel Danieli, Venice." This closed the circle of the chain.

The detective re-entered his waiting cab and drove back to Hietzing. He told the driver to halt at the corner of the street on which fronted the Thorne mansion and to wait for him there. He himself walked slowly down the quiet Street and rang the bell at the iron gate.

"You come to this house again?" asked Franz, starting back in alarm when he saw who it was that had called him to the door.

"Yes, my good friend; I want to get into this house again. But not on false pretenses this time. And before you let me in you can go upstairs and ask Mrs. Bernauer if she will receive me in her own room — in her own room, mind. But make haste; I am in a hurry." The detective's tone was calm and he strolled slowly up and down in front of the gate when he had finished speaking.

The old butler hesitated a moment, then walked into the house. When he returned, rather more quickly, he looked alarmed and his tone was very humble as he asked Muller to follow him.

When the detective entered Mrs. Bernauer's room the housekeeper rose slowly from the large armchair in front of her table. She was very pale and her eyes were full of terror. She made no move to speak, so Muller began the conversation. He put down his hat, brought up a chair and placed it near the window at which the house-keeper had been sitting. Then he sat down and motioned to her to do the same.

"You are a faithful servant, all too faithful," he began. "But you are faithful only to your master. You have no devotion for his wife."

"You are mistaken," replied the woman in a low tone.

"Perhaps, but I do not think so. One does not betray the people to whom one is devoted."

Mrs. Bernauer looked up in surprise. "What — what do you know?" she stammered.

Muller did not answer the question directly, but continued: "Mrs. Thorne had a meeting recently with a strange man. It was not their first meeting, and somehow you discovered it. But before this last meeting occurred you spoke to the lady's husband about it, and it was arranged between you that you should give him a signal which would mean to him, 'Your wife is going to the meeting.' Mrs. Thorne did go to the meeting. This happened on Monday evening at about quarter past nine. Some one, who was in the neighbourhood by chance, saw a woman's figure hurrying through the garden, down to the other street, and a moment after this, the light of this lamp in your window was seen to go out. A hand had turned down the wick — it was your hand.

"This was the signal to Mr. Thorne. The mirrors over his desk reflected in his eyes the light he could not otherwise have seen as he sat by his own window. The signal, therefore, told him that the time had come to act. This same chance watcher, who had seen the woman going through the garden, had seen the lamp go out, and now saw a man's figure hurrying down the path the woman had taken. The man as well as the woman came from this house and went in the direction of the lower end of the garden.

"A little while later a shot was heard, and the next morning Leopold Winkler was found with a bullet in his back. The crime was generally taken to be a murder for the sake of robbery. But you and I, and Mr. Herbert Thorne, know very well that it was not.

"You know this since Wednesday noon. Then it was that the idea suddenly came to you, falling like a heavy weight on your soul, the idea that Winkler might not have been killed for the sake of robbery, but because of the hatred that some one bore him. Then it was that you lost your appetite suddenly, that you drove into the city with the excuse of errands to do, in order to read the papers without being seen by any one who knew you. When you came home you searched everywhere in your master's room: you made an excuse for this search, but what you wanted to find out was whether he had left anything that could betray him. Your fright had already confused your mind. You were searching probably for the weapon from which he had fired the bullet. You did not realise that he would naturally have taken it with him and thrown it somewhere into a ravine or river beside the railway track between here and Venice. How could you think for a moment that he would leave it behind him, here in his room, or dropped in the garden? But this was doubtless due to the confusion owing to your sudden alarm and anxiety — a confusion which prevented you from realising the danger of the two peculiarly hung mirrors in Mr. Thorne's room. These should have been taken away at once. This morning my sudden appearance at the garden gate prevented you from making an examination of the place of the murder. Your swoon, after I had spoken to you in the butler's room, showed me that you were carrying a burden too heavy for your strength. Finally, this afternoon, you drove to the main telegraph office in the city, as you thought that it would be safer to telegraph Mr. Thorne from there. Your telegram was very cleverly written. But you might have spared the last sentence, the request that Mr. Thorne should get the Viennese papers of these last days. Believe me, he has already read these papers. Who could be more interested in what they have to tell than he?"

The housekeeper had sat as if frozen to stone during Muller's long speech. Her face was ashen and her eyes wild with horror. When the detective ceased speaking, there was dead silence in the room for some time. Finally Muller asked: "Is this what happened?" His voice was cutting and the glance of his eyes keen and sharp.

Mrs. Bernauer trembled. Her head sank on her breast. Muller waited a moment more and then he said quietly: "Then it is true."

"Yes, it is true," came the answer in a low hoarse tone.

Again there was silence for an appreciable interval.

"If you had been faithful to your mistress as well, if you had not spied upon her and betrayed her to her husband, all this might not have happened," continued the detective pitilessly, adding with a bitter smile: "And it was not even a case of sinful love. Your mistress had no such relations with this Winkler as you — I say this to excuse you — seemed to believe."

Adele Bernauer sprang up. "I do not need this excuse," she cried, trembling in excitement. "I do not need any excuse. What I have done I did after due consideration and in the realisation that it was absolutely necessary to do it. Never for one moment did I believe that my mistress was untrue to her husband. Never for one moment could I believe such an evil thing of her, for I knew her to be an angel of goodness. A woman who is deceiving her husband is not as unhappy as this poor lady has been for months. A woman does not write to a successful lover with so much sorrow, with so many tears. I had long suspected these meetings before I discovered them, but I knew that these meetings had nothing whatever to do with love. Because I knew this, and only because I knew it, did I tell my master about them. I wanted him to protect his wife, to free her from the wretch who had obtained some power over her, I knew not how."

"Ah! then that was it?" exclaimed Muller, and his eyes softened as he looked at the sobbing woman who had sunk back into her chair. He laid his hand on her cold fingers and continued gently: "Then you have really done right, you have done only what was your duty. I pity you deeply that you — "

"That I have brought suspicion upon my master by my own foolishness?" she finished the sentence with a pitifully sad smile. "If I could have controlled myself, could have kept calm, nobody would have had a thought or a suspicion that he — my pet, my darling — that it was he who was forced, through some terrible circumstance of which I do not know, to free his wife, in this manner, from the wretch who persecuted her."

Mrs. Bernauer wrung her hands and gazed with despairing eyes at the man who sat before her, himself deeply moved.

Again there was a long silence. Muller could not find a word to comfort the weeping woman. There was no longer anger in his heart, nothing but the deepest pity. He took out his handkerchief and wiped away the drops that were dimming his own eyes.

"You know that I will have to go to Venice?" he asked.

Mrs. Bernauer sprang up. "Officially?" she gasped, pale to her lips.

He nodded. "Yes, officially of course. I must make a report at once to headquarters about what I have learned. You can imagine yourself what the next steps will be."

Her deep sigh showed him that she knew as well as he. In the same second, however, a thought shot through her brain, changing her whole king. Her pale face glowed, her dulled eyes shot fire, and the fingers with which she held Muller's hand tightly clasped, were suddenly feverishly hot.

"And you — you are still the only person who knows the truth?" she gasped in his ear.

The detective nodded. "And you thought you might silence me?" he asked calmly. "That will not be easy — for you can imagine that I did not come unarmed."

Adele Bernauer smiled sadly. "I would take even this way to save Herbert Thorne from disgrace, if I thought that it could be successful, and if I had not thought of a milder way to silence a man who cannot be a millionaire. I have served in this house for thirty-two years, I have been treated with such generosity that I have been able to save almost every cent of my wages for my old age. With the interest that has rolled up, my little fortune must amount to nearly eight thousand gulden. I will gladly give it to you, if you will but keep silence, if you will not tell what you have discovered." She spoke gaspingly and sank down on her knees before she had finished.

"And Mr. Thorne also — " she continued hastily, as she saw no sign of interest in Muller's calm face. Then her voice failed her.

The detective looked down kindly on her grey hairs and answered: "No, no, my good woman; that won't do. One cannot conceal one crime by committing another. I myself would naturally not listen to your suggestion for a moment, but I am also convinced that Mr. Thorne, to whom you are so devoted, and who, I acknowledge, pleased me the very first sight I had of him — I am convinced that he would not agree for a moment to any such solution of the problem."

"Then I can only hope that you will not find him in Venice," replied Mrs. Bernauer, with utter despair in her voice and eyes.

"I am not at all certain that I will find him in Venice when I leave here to-morrow morning," said Muller calmly.

"Oh! then you don't want to find him! Oh God! how good, how inexpressibly good you are," stammered the woman, seizing at some vague hope in her distraught heart.

"No, you are mistaken again, Mrs. Bernauer. I will find Mr. Thorne wherever he may be. But I may arrive in Venice too late to meet him there. He may already be on his way home."

"On his way home?" cried the housekeeper in terror, staggering where she stood.

Muller led her gently to a chair. "Sit down here and listen to me calmly. This is what I mean. If Mr. Thorne has seen in the papers that a man has been arrested and accused of the murder of Leopold Winkler, then he will take the next train back and give himself up to the authorities. That he makes no such move as long as he thinks there is no suspicion on any one else, no possibility that any one else could suffer the consequences of his deed — is quite comprehensible — it is only natural and human."

Adele Bernauer sighed deeply again and heavy tears ran down her cheeks, in strange contrast to the ghost of a smile that parted her lips and shone in her dimmed eyes.

"You know him better than I do," she murmured almost inaudibly, "you know him better than I do, and I have known him for so long."

A moment later Muller had parted from the housekeeper with a warm, sincere pressure of the hand.

"Lieutenant Theobald Leining was here on a visit to his sister last March, wasn't he?" the detective asked as Franz led him out of the gate.

"Yes, sir; the Lieutenant was here just about that time," answered the old man.

"And he left here on the 16th of March?"

"On the 16th? Why, it may have been — yes, it was the 16th — that is our lady's birthday. He went away that day." Franz bowed a farewell to this stranger who began to appear uncanny in his eyes, and shutting the gate carefully he returned to the house.

"What does the man want anyway?" he murmured to himself, shivering involuntarily. Without knowing why he turned his steps towards Mrs. Bernauer's room. He opened the door hesitatingly as if afraid of what he might see there. He would not have been at all surprised if he had found the housekeeper fainting on the floor as before.

But she was not fainting this time. She was very much alive, for, to Franz's great astonishment, she was busied at the packing of a valise.

"Are you going away too?" asked Franz. Mrs. Bernauer answered in a voice that was dull with weariness: "Yes, Franz, I am going away. Will you please look up the time-tables of the Southern railroad and let me know when the morning express leaves? And please order a cab in time for it. I will depend upon you to look after the house in my absence. You can imagine that it must be something very important that takes me to Venice."

"To Venice? Why, what are you going to Venice for?"

"Never mind about that, Franz, but help me to pray that I may get there in time."

She almost pushed the old man out of the door with these last words and shut and locked it behind him.

She wanted to be alone with this hideous fear that was clutching at her heart. For it was not to Franz that she could tell the thoughts that came to her lips now as she sank down, wringing her hands, before a picture of the Madonna: "Oh Holy Virgin, Mother of our Lord, plead for me! let me be with my dear mistress when the terrible time comes and they take her husband away from her, or, if preferring death to disgrace, he ends his life by his own hand!"

CHAPTER XI. IN THE POLICE COURT

Commissioner Von Riedau sat at his desk late that evening, finishing up some important papers. The quiet of an undisturbed night watch had settled down on the busy police station. An occasional low murmur of whispering voices floated up from the guardroom below, but otherwise the stillness was broken only by the scratching of the commissioner's pen and the rustle of the paper as he turned the leaves. It was a silence so complete that a light step on the stair outside and the gentle turning of the doorknob was heard distinctly and the commissioner looked up with almost a start to see who was coming to his room so late. Joseph Muller stood in the open door, awaiting his chief's official recognition.

"Oh! it's you, Muller. So late? Come in. Anything new?" asked the commissioner. "Have you succeeded in drawing a confession from that stubborn tramp yet? You've been interviewing him, I take it?"

"Yes, I had a long talk with Johann Knoll today."

"Well, that ought to help matters along. Has he confessed? What could you get out of him?"

"Nothing, or almost nothing more than he told us here in the station, sir.

"The man's incredibly stubborn," said the

commissioner. "If he could only be made to understand that a free confession would benefit him more than any one else! Well, don't look so downcast about it, Muller. This thing is going to take longer than we thought at first for such a simple affair. But it's only a question of time until the man comes to his senses. You'll get him to talk soon. You always do. And even if you should fail here, this matter is not so very important, when we think of all the other things you have done." Muller, standing front of the desk, shook his head sadly.

"But I haven't failed here, sir. More's the pity, I had almost said."

"What!" The commissioner looked up in surprise. "I thought you just said that you couldn't get anything more out of the accused."

"Knoll has told us all he knows, sir. He did not murder Leopold Winkler."

"Hmph!" The commissioner's exclamation had a touch of acidity in it. "Then, if he didn't murder him, who did?"

"Herbert Thorne, painter, living in the Thorne mansion in B. Street, Hietzing, now in Venice, Hotel Danieli. I ask for a warrant for his arrest, sir, and orders to start for Venice on the early morning express to-morrow."

"Muller!... what the deuce does all this mean?" The commissioner sprang up, his face flushing deeply as he leaned over the desk staring at the sad quiet face of the little man opposite. "What are you talking about? What does all this mean?"

"It means, sir, that we now know who committed the murder in Hietzing. Johann Knoll is innocent of anything more than the theft confessed by himself. He took the purse and watch from the senseless form of the just murdered man. The body was warm and still supple and the tramp supposed the victim to be merely intoxicated. His story was in every respect true, sir."

The commissioner flushed still deeper. "And who do you say murdered this man?"

"Herbert Thorne, sir.

"But Thome! I know of him... have even a slight personal acquaintance with him. Thorne is a rich man, of excellent family. Why should he murder and rob an obscure clerk like this Winkler?"

"He did not rob him sir, Knoll did that."

"Oh, yes. But why should Thorne commit murder on this man who scarcely touched his life at any point... It's incredible! Muller! Muller! are you sure you are not letting your imagination run away with you again? It is a serious thing to make such an accusation against any man, much less against a man in Thorne's position. Are you sure of what you are saying?" The commissioner's excitement rendered him almost inarticulate. The shock of the surprise occasioned by the detective's words produced a feeling of irritation... a phenomenon not unusual in the minds of worthy but pedantic men of affairs when confronted by a startling new thought.

"I am quite sure of what I am saying, sir. I have just heard the confession of one who might be called an accomplice of the murderer."

"It is incredible... incredible! An accomplice you say?... who is this accomplice? Might it not be some one who has a grudge against Thorne — some one who is trying to purposely mislead you?"

"I am not so easily deceived or misled, sir. Every evidence points to Thorne, and the confession I have just heard was made by a woman who loves him, who has loved and cared for him from his babyhood. There is not the slightest doubt of it, sir."

Muller moved a step nearer the desk, gazing firmly in the eyes of the excited commissioner. The sadness on the detective's face had given way to a gleam of pride that flushed his sallow cheek and brightened his grey eyes. It was one of those rare moments when Muller allowed himself a feeling of triumph in his own power, in spite of official subordination and years of habit. His slight frame seemed to grow taller and broader as he faced the Chief with an air of quiet determination that made him at once master of the situation. His voice was as low as ever but it took on a keen incisive note that compelled attention, as he continued: "Herbert Thorne is the murderer of Leopold Winkler. Now that he knows an innocent man is under accusation for his deed it is only a question of time before he will come himself to confess. He will doubtless make this confession to me, if I go to Venice to see him, and to bring him back to trial."

The commissioner could doubt no longer. Pedantic though he was, Commissioner von Riedau possessed sufficient insight to know the truth when it was presented to him with such conviction, and also sufficient insight to have recognised the gifts of the man before him. "But why... why?" he murmured, sinking back into his chair, and shaking his head in bewilderment.

"Winkler was a miserable scoundrel, sir, a blackmailer. Thorne did only what any decent man would have felt like doing in his place. But justice must be done."

Muller's elation vanished and a deep sigh welled up from his heart. The commissioner nodded slowly, and glanced across the desk almost timidly. This case had appeared to be so simple, and suddenly the hidden deeps of a dark mystery had opened before him, deeps already sounded by the little man here who had gone so quietly about his work while the official police, represented in this case by Commissioner von Riedau himself, had sat calmly waiting for an innocent man to confess to a crime he had not committed! It was humiliating. The commissioner flushed again and his eyes sank to the floor.

"Tell me what you know, Muller," he said finally.

Muller told the story of his experiences in the Thorne mansion, told of the slight clues which led him to take an interest in the house and its inmates, until finally the truth began to glimmer up out of the depths. The commissioner listened with eager interest. "Then you believed this elaborate yarn told by the tramp?" he interrupted once, at the beginning of the narrative.

"Why, yes, sir, just because it was so elaborate. A man like Knoll would not have had the mind to invent such a story. It must have been true, on the face of it."

The commissioner's eyes sank again, and he did not speak until the detective had reached the end of his story. Then he opened a drawer in his desk and took out a bundle of official blank-forms.

"It is wonderful! Wonderful! Muller, this case will go on record as one of your finest achievements — and we thought it was so simple."

"Oh, indeed, sir, chance favoured me at every turn," replied Muller modestly.

"There is no such thing as chance," said the

commissioner. "We might as well be honest with ourselves. Any one might have seen, doubtless did see, all the things you saw, but no one else had the insight to recognise their value, nor the skill to follow them up to such a conclusion. But it's a sad case, a sad case. I never wrote a warrant with a heavier heart. Thorne is a true-hearted gentleman, while the scoundrel he killed..."

"Yes, sir, I feel that way about it myself. I can confess now that there was one moment when I was ready to-well, just to say nothing.

"And let us blunder on in our official stupidity and blindness?" interrupted the commissioner, a faint smile breaking the gravity of his face. "We certainly gave you every opportunity."

"But there's an innocent man accused — suffering fear of death — justice must be done. But, sir," Muller took the warrant the commissioner handed across the table to him. "May I not make it as easy as I can for Mr. Thorne — I mean, bring him here with as little publicity as possible? His wife is with him in Venice."

"Poor little woman, it's terrible! Do whatever you think best, Muller. You're a queer mixture. Here you've hounded this man down, followed hot on his trail when not a soul but yourself connected him in any way with the murder. And now you're sorry for him! A soft heart like yours is a dangerous possession for a police detective, Muller. It's no aid to our business."

"No, sir, I know that."

"Well take care it doesn't run away with you this time. Don't let Herbert Thorne escape, however much pity you may feel for him."

"I doubt if he'll want to sir, as long as another is in prison for his crime.

"But he may make his confession and then try to escape the disgrace."

"Yes, sir, I've thought of that. That's why I want to go to Venice myself. And then, there's the poor young wife, he must think of her when the desire comes to end his own life..."

"Yes! Yes! This terrible thing has shaken us both up more than a little. I feel exhausted. You look tired yourself, Muller. Go home now, and get some rest for your early start. Good-night."

"Good-night, sir."

CHAPTER XII. ON THE LIDO

A Wonderfully beautiful night lay over the fair old city of Venice when the Northern Express thundered over the long bridge to the railway station. A passenger who was alone in a second-class compartment stood up to collect his few belongings. Suddenly he looked up as he heard a voice, a voice which he had learned to know only very recently, calling to him from the door of the compartment.

"Why! you were in the train too? You have come to Venice?" exclaimed Joseph Muller in astonishment as he saw Mrs. Bernauer standing there before him.

"Yes, I have come to Venice too. I must be with my dear lady — when — when Herbert — " She had begun quite calmly, but she did not finish her sentence, for loud sobs drowned the words.

"You were in the next compartment? Why didn't you come in here with me? It would have made this journey shorter for both of us."

"I had to be alone," said the pale woman and then she added: "I only came to you now to ask you where I must go."

"I think we two had better go to the Hotel Bauer. Let me arrange things for you. Mrs. Thorne must not see you until she has been prepared for your coming. I will arrange that with her husband."

The two took each other's hands. They had won respect and sympathy for each other, this quiet man who went so relentlessly and yet so pityingly about his duty in the interest of justice — and the devoted woman whose faithfulness had brought about such a tragedy.

The train had now entered the railway station. Muller and Mrs. Bernauer stood a few minutes later on the banks of the Grand Canal and entered, one of the many gondolas waiting there. The moon glanced back from the surface of the water broken into ripples under the oars of the gondoliers; it shone with a magic charm on the old palaces that stood knee-deep in the lagoons, and threw heavy shadows over the narrow water-roads on which the little dark boats glided silently forward. In most of the gondolas coming from the station excited voices and exclamations of delight broke the calm of the moonlit evening as the tourists rejoiced in the beauty that is Venice.

But in the gondola in which Muller and Mrs. Bernauer sat there was deep silence, silence broken only by a sobbing sigh that now and then burst from the heart of the haggard woman. There were few travellers entering Venice on one of its world-famous moonlit nights who were so sad at heart as were these two.

And there were few travellers in Venice as

heavy hearted as was the man who next morning took one of the earliest boats out to the Lido.

Muller and Mrs. Bernauer were on the same boat watching him from a hidden corner. The woman's sad eyes gazed yearningly at the haggard face of the tall man who stood looking over the railing of the little steamer. Her own tears came as she saw the gloom in the once shining grey eyes she loved so well.

Muller stood beside Mrs. Bernauer. His eyes too, keen and quick, followed Herbert Thorne as he stood by the rail or paced restlessly up and down; his face too showed pity and concern. He also saw that Thorne held in his hand a bundle of newspapers which were still enclosed in their mailing wrappers. The papers were pressed in a convulsive grip of the artist's long slender fingers.

Muller knew then that Thorne had not yet learned of the arrest of Johann Knoll. At the very earliest, Thursday's papers, which brought the news, could not reach him before Friday morning. But these newspapers (Muller saw that they were German papers) were still in their wrappings. They were probably Viennese papers for which he had telegraphed and which had just arrived. His anxiety had not allowed him to read them in the presence of his wife. He had sought the solitude of early morning on the Lido, that he might learn, unobserved, what terrors fate had in store for him.

It was doubtless Mrs. Bernauer's telegram which caused his present anxiety, a telegram which had reached him only the night before when he returned with his wife from an excursion to Torcello. It had caused him a sleepless night, for it had brought the realisation that his faithful nurse suspected the truth about the murder in the quiet lane. The telegram had read as follows: "Have drawn money and send it at once. Further journey probably necessary, visitor in house to-day. Connected with occurrence in — Street. Please read Viennese papers. News and orders for me please send to address A.B. General Postoffice."

This telegram told Herbert Thorne the truth. And the papers which arrived this morning were to tell him more — what he did not yet know. But his heart was drawn with terrors which threw lines in his face and made him look ten years older than on that Tuesday morning when the detective saw him setting out on his journey with his wife.

When the boat landed at the Lido, Thorne walked off down the road which led to the ocean side. Muller and Mrs. Bernauer entered the waiting tramway that took them in the same direction. They dismounted in front of the bathing establishment, stepped behind a group of bushes and waited there for Thorne. In about ten minutes they saw his tall figure passing on the other side of the road. He was walking down to the beach, holding the still unopened papers in his hand.

A narrow strip of park runs along parallel to the beach in the direction towards Mala Mocco. Muller and Mrs Bernauer walked along through this park on the path which was nearest the water. The detective watched the rapidly moving figure ahead of them, while the woman's tear-dimmed eyes veiled everything else to her but the path along which her weary feet hastened. Thorne halted about half way between the bathing establishment and the customs barracks, looked around to see if he were alone and threw himself down on the sand.

He had chosen a good place. To the right and to the left were high sand dunes, before him was the broad surface of the ocean, and at his back was rising ground, bare sand with here and there a scraggly bush or a group of high thistles. Herbert Thorne believed himself to be alone here... as far as a man can be alone over whom hangs the shadow of a crime. He groaned aloud and hid his pale face in his hands.

In his own distress he did not hear the deep sigh — which, just above him on the edge of the knoll, broke from the breast of a woman who was suffering scarcely less than he; he did not know that two pair of sad eyes looked down upon him. And now into the eyes of the watching woman there shot a gleam of terror. For Herbert Thorne had taken a revolver from his pocket and laid it quietly beside him. Then he took out a notebook and a pencil and placed them beside the weapon. Then slowly, reluctantly, he opened one of the papers.

A light breeze from the shining sea before him carried off the wrapping. The paper which he opened shook in his trembling hands, as his eyes sought the reports of the murder. He gave a sudden start and a tremor ran through his frame. He had come to the spot which told of the arrest of another man, who was under shadow of punishment for the crime which he himself had committed. When he had read this report through, he turned to the other papers. He was quite calm now, outwardly calm at least.

When he had finished reading the papers he laid them in a heap beside him and reached out for his notebook. As he opened it the two watchers saw that between its first pages there was a sealed and addressed letter. Two other envelopes were contained in the notebook, envelopes which were also addressed although still open. Muller's sharp eyes could read the addresses as Thorne took them up in turn, looking long at each of them. One envelope was addressed in Italian to the Chief of Police of Venice, the other to the Chief of Police in Vienna.

The two watchers leaned forward, scarcely three yards above the man in whom they were interested. Thorne tore out two leaves of his notebook and wrote several lines on each of them.

One note, he placed in the envelope addressed to the Viennese police and sealed it carefully. Then he put the sealed letter with the second note in the other envelope, the one addressed to the Italian police. He put all the letters back in his notebook, holding it together with a rubber strap, and replaced it in his pocket.

Then he stretched out his hand toward the revolver.

The sand came rattling down upon him, the thistles bent over creakingly and two figures appeared beside him.

"There's time enough for that yet, Mr. Thorne," said the man at whom the painter gazed up in bewilderment. And then this man took the revolver quietly from his hand and hid it in his own pocket.

Thorne pressed his teeth down on his lips until the blood came. He could not speak; he looked first at the stranger who had mastered him so completely, and then, in dazed astonishment, at the woman who had sunk down beside him in the sand, clasping his hand in both of hers.

"Adele! Adele! 'Why are you here?" he stammered finally.

"I want to be with you — in this hour," she answered, looking at him with eyes of worship. "I want to be with my dear lady — to comfort her — to protect her when — when — "

"When they arrest me?" Thorne finished the sentence himself. Then turning to Muller he continued: "And that is why you are here?"

"Yes, Mr. Thorne. I have a warrant for your arrest in my pocket. But I think it will be unnecessary to make use of it in the customary official way through the authorities here. I see that you have written to both police stations — confessing your deed. This will amount to a voluntary giving up of yourself to the authorities, therefore all that is necessary is that I return with you in the same train which takes you to Vienna. But I must ask you for those two letters, for until you yourself give them to the police authorities in my presence, it is my duty to keep them."

Muller had seldom found his official duty as difficult as it was now. His words came haltingly and great drops stood out on his forehead.

The painter rose from the sand and he too wiped his face, which was drawn in agony.

"Herbert, Herbert!" cried Adele Bernauer suddenly. "Oh, Herbert, you will live, you will! Promise me, you will not think of suicide, it would kill your wife — "

She lay on her knees before him in the sand. He looked down at her gently and with a gesture which seemed to be a familiar one of days long past, he stroked the face that had grown old and worn in these hours of fear for him.

"Yes, you dear good soul, I will live on, I will take upon myself my punishment for killing a scoundrel. The poor man whom they have arrested in my place must not linger in the fear of death. I am ready, sir.

"My name is Muller — detective Muller."

"Joseph Muller, the famous detective Muller?" asked Thorne with a sad smile. "I have had little to do with the police but by chance I have heard of your fame. I might have known; they tell me you are one from whom the truth can never remain hidden."

"My duty is not always an easy one," said Muller.

"Thank you. Dispose of me as you will. I do not wish any privileges that others would not have, Mr. Muller. Here is my written confession and here am I myself. Shall we go now?" Herbert Thorne handed the detective his notebook with its important contents and then walked slowly back along the road he had come.

Muller walked a little behind him, while Mrs. Bernauer was at his side. As in days long past, they walked hand in hand.

With eyes full of pity Muller watched them, and he heard Thorne give his old nurse orders for the care of his wife. She was to take Mrs. Thorne to Graz to her father, then to return herself to Vienna and take care of the house as usual, until his attorney could settle up his affairs and sell the property. For Thorne said that neither he nor his wife would ever want to set foot in the house again. He spoke calmly, he thought of everything — he thought even of the possibility that he might have to pay the death penalty for his deed.

For who could tell how the authorities would judge this murder?

It had indeed been a murder by merest chance only. Thorne told his old nurse all about it. When she had given him the signal he had hurried down into the garden, and walking quietly along the path, he had found his wife at the garden gate in conversation with a man who was a stranger to him. That part of their talk which he overheard told him that the man was a blackmailer, and that he was making money on the fact that he had caught Theobald Leining cheating at cards.

This chance had put the officer into Winkler's power. The clerk knew that he could get nothing from the guilty man himself, so he had turned to the latter's sister, who was rich, and had threatened to bring about a disgraceful scandal if she did not pay for his silence. For more than a year he had been getting money from her by means of these threats. All this was clear from the conversation. The man spoke in tones of impertinence, or sneering obsequiousness, the woman s voice showed contempt and hatred.

Thorne's blood began to boil. His fingers tightened about the revolver which he had brought with him to be ready for any emergency, and he stepped designedly upon a twig which broke under his feet with a noise. He wanted to frighten his wife and send her back to the house. This was what did occur. But the blackmailer was alarmed as well and fled hastily from the garden when he realised that he was not alone with his victim. Thorne followed the man's disappearing figure, calling him to halt. He did not call loudly for he too wanted to avoid a scandal. His intention was to force the man to follow him into the house, to get his written confession of blackmail — then to finish him off with a large sum once for all and kick him out of the place.

In this manner Herbert Thorne thought to free himself and his wife from the persecutions of the rascal. His heart was filled with hatred towards the man. For since Mrs. Bernauer had told him what she had discovered, he knew that it was because of this wretch that his once so happy wife was losing her strength, her health and her peace of mind.

He followed the fleeing man and called to him several times to halt. Finally Winkler half turned and called out over his shoulder: "You'd better leave me alone! Do you want all Vienna to know that your brother-in-law ought to be in jail?"

These words robbed Thorne of all control.

He pressed the trigger under his finger and the bullet struck the man before him, who had turned to continue his flight, full in the back. "And that is how I became a murderer." With these words Herbert Thorne concluded his narrative. He appeared quite calm now. He was really calmer, for the strain of the deed, which was justified in his eyes, was not so great upon his conscience as had been the strain of the secret of it.

In his own eyes he had only killed a beast who chanced to bear the form of a man. But of course in the eyes of the world this was a murder like any other, and the man who had committed it knew that he was under the ban of the law, that it was only a chance that the arm of justice had not yet reached out for him. And now this arm had reached out for him, although it was no longer necessary. For Herbert Thorne was not the man to allow another to suffer in his stead.

As soon as he knew that another had been arrested and was under suspicion of the murder, he knew that there was nothing more for him but open confession. But he wished to avoid a scandal even now. If he died by his own hand, then the first cause of all this trouble, his brother-in-law's rascality, could still be hidden.

But now his care was all in vain and Herbert Thorne knew that he must submit to the inevitable. Side by side with his old friend he sat on the deck of the boat that took them back to the Riva dei Schiavoni. Muller sat at some distance from them. The pale sad-faced woman, and the pale sad-faced man had much to say to each other that a stranger might not hear.

When the little boat reached the landing stage, there were but a few steps more to the door of the Hotel Danieli. From a balcony on the first floor a young woman stood looking down onto the canal. She too was pale and her eyes were heavy with anxiety. She had been pale and anxious even then, the day when she left the beautiful old house in the quiet street, to start on this pleasure trip to Venice.

It had been no pleasure trip to her. She had seen the change in her husband, a change that struck deep into his very being and altered him in everything except in his love and tender care for her. "Oh, why is it? what is the matter?" she asked her self a thousand times a day. Could it be possible that he had discovered the secret which tortured her, the only secret she had ever had from him, the secret she had longed to confess to him a hundred times but had lacked courage to do it.

For she had sinned deeply against her husband, she knew. Her fear and her confusion had driven her deeper and deeper into the waters of deceit until it was impossible for her to find the words that would have brought help and comfort from the man whom she loved more than anything else in the world. In the very earliest stages of Winkler's persecution she had lost her head completely and instead of confessing to her husband and asking for his aid and protection, she had pawned the rich jewels which had been his wedding present to get the money demanded by the blackmailer. In her ignorance she had thought that this one sum would satisfy him.

But he came again and again, demanding money which she saved from her pin money, from her household allowance, thus taking what she had intended to use to redeem her jewels. The pledge was lost, and her jewels gone forever. From now on, Mrs. Thorne lived in a terror which sapped her strength and drank her life blood drop by drop. Any hour might bring discovery, a discovery which she feared would shake her husband's love for her. The poor weak little woman grew pale and ill. She wrote finally to her stepbrother, but he could think of no way out; he wrote only that if the matter came to a scandal there would be nothing for him to do but to kill himself. This was one reason more for her silence, and Mrs. Thorne faded to a wan shadow of her former sunny self.

As she looked down from the balcony, she was like a woman suffering from a deathly illness. A new terror had come to her heart because her husband had gone away so early without telling her why or whither he had gone. When she saw him coming towards the door of the hotel, pale and drooping, and when she saw Mrs. Bernauer beside him, her heart seemed to stand still. She crept back from the window and stood in the middle of the room as Herbert Thorne and his former nurse entered.

"What has happened?" This was all she could say as she looked into the distraught face of the housekeeper, into her husband's sad eyes.

He led her to a chair, then knelt beside her and told her all.

"Outside the door stands the man who will take me back to Vienna — and you, my dearest, you must go to your father." He concluded his story with these words.

She bent down over him and kissed him. "'No, I am going with you," she said softly, strangely calm; "why should I leave you now? Is it not I who am the cause of this dreadful thing?"

And then she made her confession, much too late. And she went with him, back to the city of their home. It seemed to them both quite natural that she should do so.

When the Northern Express rolled out of Venice that afternoon, three people sat together in a compartment, the curtains of which were drawn close. They were the unhappy couple and their faithful servant. And outside in the corridor of the railway carriage, a small, slight man walked up and down — up and down. He had pressed a gold coin into the conductor's hand, with the words: "The party in there do not wish to be disturbed; the lady is ill."

Herbert Thorne's trial took place several weeks later. Every possible extenuating circumstance was brought to bear upon his sentence. Five years only was to be the term of his imprisonment, his punishment for the crime of a single moment of anger.

His wife waited for him in patient love. She did not go to Graz, but continued to live in the old mansion with the mansard roof. Her father was with her. The brother Theobald, the cause of all this suffering to those who had shielded him at the expense of their own happiness, had at last done the only good deed of his life — had put an end to his useless existence with his own hand.

Father and daughter waited patiently for the return of the man who had sinned and suffered for their sake. They spoke of him only in terms of the tenderest affection and respect.

And indeed, seldom has any condemned murderer met with the respect of the entire community as Herbert Thorne did. The tone of the newspapers, and public opinion, evinced by hundreds of letters from friends, acquaintances, and from strangers, was a great boon to the solitary man in his cell, and to the three loving hearts in the old house. And at the end of two years the clemency of the Monarch ended his term of imprisonment, and Herbert Thorne was set free, a step which met with the approval of the entire city.

He returned to the home where love and affection awaited him, ready to make him forget what he had suffered. But the silver threads in his dark hair and a certain quiet seriousness in his manner, and in the hearts of all the dwellers in the old mansion, showed that the occurrence of that fatal 27th of September had thrown a shadow over them all which was not to be shaken off.

Joseph Muller brought many other cases to a successful solution. But for years after this particular case had been won, he was followed, as by a shadow, by a man who watched over him, and who, whenever danger threatened, stood over the frail detective as if to take the blow upon himself. He is a clever assistant, too, and no one who had seen Johann Knoll the day that he was put into the cell on suspicion of murder would have believed that the idle tramp could become again such a useful member of society. These are the victories that Joseph Muller considers his greatest.